Sherlock Holmes
at
The Raffles Hotel

John Hall

A Sherlock Holmes murder mystery
First published in 2008
under the Breese Books imprint by
The Irregular Special Press
for Baker Street Studios Ltd
Endeavour House
170 Woodland Road, Sawston
Cambridge CB22 3DX, UK

ISBN: 1-901091-32-5 (10 digit)
ISBN: 978-1-901091-32-8 (13 digit)

Cover Concept: Antony J. Richards

Cover Illustration: The Raffles Hotel, including a clue on the back cover, from an
original watercolour by Nikki Sims.

Typeset in 8/11/20pt Palatino

This book is dedicated to the founders of the Raffles Hotel, the
four Sarkies brothers:
Martin, Tigran, Aviet and Arshak

By the same author and published by Breese Books

Sherlock Holmes and The Abbey School Mystery
Sherlock Holmes and The Adler Papers
Sherlock Holmes and The Boulevard Assassin
Sherlock Holmes and The Disgraced Inspector
Sherlock Holmes and The Hammerford Will
Sherlock Holmes and The Telephone Murder Mystery
Special Commission
The Travels of Sherlock Holmes

Chapter One

I Received an Urgent Summons ...

In the early part of the year 1905, I was at a low ebb. My second wife had died in tragic circumstances eighteen months before, and I had been unable to concentrate as I ought on my medical practice. This had led to my losing some of my former patients – to competitors in the medical field, I hasten to add, not to the 'Grim Reaper'. And that in turn had perhaps gone to make me yet more cynical, and hence more lackadaisical about my work. In a word, I was becoming convinced that Dr John H. Watson, general practitioner, writer, and biographer of the world's first consulting detective, had about come to the end of his useful working life. I felt that I was ready to retire, to sell my practice for what it would make, and do as my old friend Mr Sherlock Holmes had done, sever all links with a world that was fast becoming uncongenial to me.

On the particular morning of which I write, I had sat in my little consulting room waiting for patients. Waiting without result, for I had not a single call upon my professional services all the three or four hours that I sat there. I sat there, trying to read

The Lancet, or some more popular journal as the fancy took me, but unable to concentrate even on the most frivolous of articles. And after a minute or two trying to read and failing, I would put down whatever magazine I had just taken up, and stare out of the window at the grey London around me. There was a thin drizzle falling, and I could see rivulets of rain trickling down the outside of the window; so melancholy was I that it seemed to me that I was seeing the last years of my life trickling, useless, into the great ocean of nothingness.

At ten-thirty I had a word with the maid and popped round to the bank, drawing out some money for the week's expenditure – a fortunate circumstance, as you shall see.

When I returned, there had been no callers, nor were there any in the hour or so that immediately followed my return. At a little before noon I had had enough, I could stand the monotony no longer, and so I determined on an earlier luncheon than was usual with me. I took my hat, coat and stick, called out to the maid that I should be back in an hour or so, and marched to the front door.

As I pulled the door open, a young lad in the uniform of a messenger boy was just about to ring at the bell, and I caught him off balance. He quickly recovered his footing, touched his cap, and asked me, "Doctor Watson, is it, sir?"

"Yes, indeed."

"Telegram, Doctor." And he held out the little square, buff-coloured envelope.

"Ahah! An urgent case, perhaps?" My spirits rose at the prospect, and I tore the envelope open, taking in the contents at a glance.

It was signed by Martha, the elderly and respectable lady who acted as housekeeper for Mr Sherlock Holmes at his little cottage on the Sussex coast, and it read thus:

> Mr Holmes very bad.
> Can you come at once?

"No reply," I told the lad, handing him what I thought was a shilling.

"Thank *you*, sir." He touched his cap, and I realized it had been a half-crown; but what of it? The main thing now was to get to Holmes, and that without any undue delay!

I mentioned the telegram to the maid, giving her the address at which I might be contacted and leaving some instructions in the event that a sudden crowd of patients should come knocking at my door. A word to my near neighbour, Anstruther, who looked after my practice – such as it was – in life's little emergencies, completed that side of the arrangements. And then a few minutes spent packing the bare essentials for the journey, and picking up my stethoscope and what have you, and in less than a quarter of an hour after opening the fateful telegram, I was in a cab on my way to the railway station.

An hour later, I was sitting in a first-class carriage, staring aimlessly out of the window, down which the rain still coursed, though in a more lively fashion now, as the passage of the speeding train produced its own little gale. I sat there, alone in my compartment at that time of day and that season of the year, my mind totally occupied with thoughts of Holmes, as the train headed through the grey weather towards Brighton.

Holmes's little cottage – his 'villa', as he dignifies it, with modest pride – is a mile from the little village of Fulworth, itself at no great distance from Brighton, that seaside resort so beloved of Londoners. I had visited Holmes on several occasions before, and on many of these visits, the weather being fine, I had walked from the station to his cottage, enjoying scenery and fresh air alike.

Today, however, time seemed to be ebbing away from me, I had the wildest fears and fancies as to what might not be happening in that lonely cottage on the high downs. Moreover, the rain had still not entirely abated. Accordingly, I hired a pony and trap at Brighton, and drove into Fulworth village. The path to Holmes' cottage is a steep one, too steep for the poor pony, so I did as I had done on a couple of previous visits, and left pony and cart at the local inn, to be collected later.

Never did that cliff-side path seem so steep, so slippery, or so long. I hastened as I have seldom hastened before, the drizzle soaking in a most insidious manner into my clothing. It was growing dark as I passed Holmes' nearest neighbours at The Gables, some sort of school, as I understood it from Holmes. They were lighting their lamps there as I scurried past the gate, and the friendly cheerful glow seemed to mock my damp and miserable condition.

Another half mile through the damp turf, my boots ruined, my trouser legs soaked, and there stood Holmes' little cottage. Some sort of creeper, now bare of leaves, circled round the door, and in my sombre mood it seemed like an icy tentacle round a man's heart. A few pots, empty of plants, seemed to reflect the emptiness of existence; and the little beehives, the study of which had latterly engaged all of Holmes' attention as readily and as deeply as the study of London's underworld had once engaged it, stood silent and forlorn, their occupants presumably still deep in their winter slumbers.

Worst of all, the place was in total darkness. The blinds were down, the curtains closed, not a lamp, nor a candle, nor a match was lit. Fool that I was, I ought to have known – easy enough to say, with hindsight, of course. If Holmes had indeed been gravely ill, so ill as to warrant the sending of a telegram to me in London, then of course old Martha would never rely solely on my going down there. She would send for a local medical man.

I reproached myself bitterly, as I made for the door, the darkness closing in on me. It should have been I, not some stranger, who attended Holmes in his hour of need. He had never looked after himself properly, had always disregarded the dictates of medical advice and common sense alike, and this was the result! I had done what I could, of course, when we shared rooms, but latterly I had all but forgotten him, who had once been my best, my only, friend. I ought to have made it my business to visit him regularly, give him good advice – and, more to the point, make sure that he took it. Instead, some young whippersnapper, fresh from medical school, had prodded and probed my old friend, doubtless made entirely the wrong diagnosis, and packed Holmes off to the hospital in Lewes, or perhaps Brighton, from whence I had just come. It was not to be thought of – Holmes, once so hale and hearty, Holmes, who could twist a poker into a knot with his bare hands, Holmes, who had thrown Moriarty over the falls at Reichenbach, Holmes who could go days without food, Holmes, my old friend, Holmes, in hospital.

That, or worse.

That, or worse!

The dreadful thought chilled me more than the rain, unmanned me more than the growing darkness. I had to stop in my tracks, my heart pounding, and make a deliberate effort to calm myself down. Hindsight, that good familiar creature, came to my aid once more, telling me that I should have knocked at the door of The Gables, for they would have been sure to know just what was going on and would tell me if Holmes had indeed been moved to hospital, or – or anything of the sort. Well, I was but a few paces from his own door now, I might just as well try here first. If I had no reply, I would retrace my steps to The Gables, make enquiries, and very likely beg the favour of a bed, even if it were on their billiard table, they would surely not be so heartless as to refuse me under these grim circumstances.

I took the last few yards in a couple of giant strides, and pounded upon the little door, loud enough, I thought without humour, to wake the dead. There came no answer. I pounded again, louder this time, and I fancy that I called out, though I could not tell you what I said.

And then, and then, came a light. A blessed light, from inside that darkened place. Through the little window at the side of the door I could see that a match was struck, a candle – no, a lamp – was lit, and the yellow glow came closer.

Then I was thunderstruck to hear Holmes' own voice. "I shall see to it, Martha," he called out, sounding for all the world as hale and hearty as ever.

The light dazzled me as the door was flung open. "Yes? What is it? A case, perhaps?" It was Holmes, Holmes himself, alive and well. Looking, perhaps, a touch thinner, a little paler, than when I had last seen him, too long ago, now, but alive and well at the very least.

He stared at me. "Watson?"

And I stared back in my turn. "Holmes?"

"Well, at least that is established, Doctor." His voice had lost none of its edge. "What is it, Watson? You look as if you'd seen a ghost, man. Come inside, and tell me all about it. You have some luggage there? You plan to stay?"

"Well ... that is ... if I may?" I shook myself, like a wet dog, and not just because of the rain that trickled down my neck. "Holmes, enough of this nonsense. Are you quite well?"

Holmes leaned towards me, and sniffed delicately. "H'mm. You have not been drinking, and your eyes indicate that you have not prescribed strong opiates for yourself ..."

"Really, Holmes!"

"... and so I deduce some powerful mental disturbance. Now, I know you well enough to believe that if it were a case, an investigation requiring my own limited talents and abilities, you would at once have blurted out such details as you knew. Incoherently, it is true, and with a fine disregard for the essentials, but you would have blurted it out ..."

"Holmes, you go too far."

"... and thus I conclude that it is something entirely out of the ordinary that brings you here." He held out his hand, and I shook it mechanically. "Come inside, Doctor, and cease to drip upon my doorstep in that unruly fashion. Remove your wet coat and hat ... the shoes, I fear, are beyond hope, but there are some slippers in the corner there ... and then take a glass of brandy and hot water, and thaw out a little by the fire."

He led me into an inner room, and I saw that there was indeed a good fire going in the grate. And through a partly open door I saw the lights of the kitchen, heard homely sounds and smelled food cooking, and caught a glimpse of old Martha. I realized, firstly that I was very hungry, having not thought about food since I decided on an early lunch, which I had entirely forgotten to have, and secondly that if I had gone to the back of the cottage, I should have seen the kitchen lights and not been quite so alarmed as I had been.

Feeling a little foolish, I allowed Holmes to take my coat,

hat and bags. "I say, though, Holmes, are you quite well?"

"Well enough, Doctor." He gazed at me quizzically. "And why do you ask that?"

By way of an answer, I produced the crumpled telegram from my pocket and handed it to him. Holmes took it in with a quick, alert glance, then turned and called out, "Martha!"

There came no response, and after a minute or two Holmes went to the door that led on to the kitchen, calling out once again, "Martha? Could you come in here a moment, please?"

The door opened, and Holmes' old housekeeper appeared. Martha was a short, stout lady, not entirely unlike the late Queen Victoria in general appearance, and like the late Queen she favoured black for her costume. Martha entered the little parlour, reluctantly as it seemed to me, glanced at Holmes, and then at me, and seemed indeed quite taken aback that I should be standing there by the fire, for she staggered slightly, and put a hand to her forehead in a somewhat theatrical manner.

"Why, if it isn't Doctor Watson," she said at once. "What a surprise. But how nice to see you again, sir. You'll be staying a day or so, I take it? I must have had some sort of premonition that you were coming, sir, for I've done easily twice as much as would feed Mr Holmes here. Sit down, gentlemen, and I'll serve the supper at once."

"Come now, Martha," said Holmes, in a tone of mock severity. He brandished the telegram at her in an accusing fashion. "Your little scheme is revealed. The good doctor here, in his usual robust manner, has, in the argot of fifty years ago, 'blown the gaff'. In a word, Martha, your surprise is a sham. You are yourself responsible for Watson's being here, and you must explain things to us."

"Well, then, sir, I'll tell you straight that I did send that telegram, and there's no use denying it. I went down to Fulworth and saw Abigail Oldwhistle, her that keeps the little draper's shop, for I knew she was bound for Brighton this morning, and that's how I did it." And Martha folded her arms and regarded Holmes complacently.

"I was less concerned with *how*, and more with the *why* of the thing," said Holmes.

"Well, sir," said Martha obstinately, "just as I can't deny that I sent that telegram there, so you can't deny that you haven't been looking after yourself properly of late, nor can you deny that you're not as well, not to say as lively, as you ought to be. The Doctor himself will say the same, I'm sure, when he's had a chance to look at you."

Holmes made as if to protest at this, but I got in first. "Ah, yes. Martha, you just take yourself off for a moment, would you, whilst I have a look at Mr Holmes? Holmes, remove your tie and unfasten your shirt."

"Really, Doctor, this is quite ..."

"Say, 'Ah', please."

"Watson ..."

"And cough."

I gave Holmes a pretty thorough examination, and could find absolutely nothing amiss. "H'mm. Heart and lungs quite sound. You could stand to put on a few pounds more in weight, but you never were what I'd call hefty." I put my stethoscope away, and metaphorically scratched my head. "I really am at a loss to understand why Martha should have sent that telegram, Holmes. Not that I'm not pleased to see you. You'll not object, I trust, if I lodge here a day or so? Not that I'm worried about you, dear fellow, but, truth to tell, I could use a short break from London myself just now."

"Ah, London." A curious look came into Holmes' eyes.

Then he shook himself. "Stay? Of course you must stay, my dear Watson. I'll have Martha make up the bed in the spare room."

"No need, sir," said Martha, who by that curious female process of divination had realized that my examination of Holmes was complete, and put her head round the kitchen door. "No need, for I did that yesterday, and set a hot water bottle in the bed to warm it last night. Now, if you'll sit down at the table, sir, I'll serve supper."

I confess that I was ready for my supper, for it had been a long day, a worrying day, and I had been too bothered to eat anything since my breakfast. I took the opportunity to study Holmes, and was somewhat concerned to see that he was merely pushing the food around his plate, evidently making a show of eating for my sake, but not really taking any sustenance. I knew well enough that this was his way when he had some knotty problem, some tricky investigation, in hand; indeed, I had protested to him about it often enough. But when he had no such case to bother about, his appetite, though never on a Rabelaisian scale, was usually hearty enough to satisfy any medical man.

I determined to sound him out. "There must be some interesting little local problems to occupy you, Holmes?" I ventured.

He raised his head, with what looked like an effort, and regarded me with lacklustre eyes.

"Doubtless you have some intriguing little matter, if not two or three, in hand just now?" I ploughed on.

For answer, Holmes made a sound remarkably like, 'Huh!' and lowered his eyes to his plate again.

"You know, Holmes," I went on, as if I had not heard this, "I am quite concerned about that telegram ..."

At which point, Holmes said something which may have been, 'Darn the telegram!' but again I chose to ignore him.

"I am wondering, since there is nothing wrong with you, whether Martha may not be ... well, not quite as sound in her grip of things as when she was younger. Do you think ..."

"I think there is nothing wrong with Martha's mind, and nor do you. She was merely exercising her feminine prerogative, and interfering in matters which are no concern of hers," said Holmes, with a good deal more spirit than he had shown thus far.

"My dear fellow, it can scarcely be called meddling, if she is so worried about you that she needs must consult me" I put down my knife and fork, and spoke as earnestly as I could. "Holmes, we have known one another now for a very long time. Will you not trust me in this, rely upon my discretion and my goodwill? To be blunt, will you not confide in me, if there is something bothering you?"

"Well, then, I had a few twinges, some months back, which the local doctor diagnosed as rheumatism."

"Is it bothering you just now?"

"No."

"Of course, it is annoying to think that one is growing old," I told him, "and rheumatism can be a nuisance. But I cannot think that it is just that which caused Martha to consult me on your behalf. Is there really nothing more, nothing that I might be able to help with?"

Holmes sat there, regarding me in silence, for very long time. Then he smiled. "It is the old enemy, Doctor."

"Not ..."

Holmes shook his head. "If I am weary it is not from some artificial cause, some noxious drug, but rather the all too natural consequence of boredom, of rank, mind-numbing stagnation. Oh, I have my little garden, and my bees; indeed, I am in the throes of writing a monograph upon the art of bee-keeping which shall be the last word on the subject. But, whilst that is all very well in summer, when plants and bees alike are busy about their lives, it is somewhat different in this cold and wet season. You see me, Watson, at the end of some six months of inactivity. Though ... a fortnight ago I was consulted by a local man about the raids on his hen house; he was convinced it was a fox though no fowls had been killed, and wanted expert advice. I saw at a glance that it was no fox, but a naughty schoolboy, after an egg or two to form the basis of an unauthorized supper in the dormitory; more, I could identify the culprit at once as being one of the young pupils at The Gables. But, naturally, I could not say as much, for it would have been unsporting. Publicly I had to admit defeat; privately, I had to be satisfied with taking the lad aside and giving him a severe lecture on the evils of petty theft and the dangers to one's digestion of eating after 'lights out'. That, Doctor, is the extent to which my deductive powers have been tested of late. Can you wonder, then, that I am listless, have no appetite, that Martha is so concerned that she calls you away from your work and your patients?"

"My work? Huh!"

Holmes ceased his lamentations, and looked at me with some sympathy. "You, too, Watson?"

"Oh, I grow old, Holmes. Old and weary, like you."

"Well, I would perhaps not say *old*, exactly," Holmes told me, with some return of his former asperity.

"Things are not the same, Holmes. A man needs work, if he is to enjoy life properly, and my own work has become tiresome. My case is not entirely dissimilar to yours; I am faced with patients whose only complaint is that ... at the end of winter … they have a runny nose and a cough. To be sure, it is a compliment to a doctor to think that his patients are so healthy that they can dispense with his services, but it scarcely makes for an interesting day."

Holmes nodded. "Then you will know exactly how things are with me. Beyond even your medical skills, I fear, Watson. Yes, our cases are remarkably similar, my boy. And, speaking of cases, I was thinking just the other day about that curious little problem of the *Beryl Coronet*, and its subsequent ramifications. I don't think you ever heard the real outcome of that one, did you? Well …" and off he went, happily reminiscing about the good old days when he was in practice in Baker Street.

I encouraged him in this search for lost time, prompting him with reflections of my own on this old case and that one; and I was considerably cheered to see that, in the intervals of reminiscing, Holmes actually made a reasonably good attack on the food in front of him.

When we had finished our dinner we sat by the fire, smoking our pipes and still yarning about the strange folk we had encountered, and their even stranger little problems, until it was woefully late.

Holmes noticed my badly stifled yawns, and apologized for keeping me up, saying with a wicked grin that I must have had a most disturbing day, that it was dangerous for an old fellow like me to hear too often the chimes at midnight, and that I would be ready for my bed. I could not argue with him, and in a very short while I was snugly tucked up in the spare bedroom, and knew no more that night.

Chapter Two

... and a Generous Invitation

I woke on the following morning, at a somewhat later hour than the critical might forgive, and found that the rain had stopped and that an unseasonable sunshine was lighting up the pattern on the chintz curtains – the latter being old Martha's choice, I felt sure, rather than Holmes'. I got out of bed, flung the curtains aside, the window open, and took a great breath of the glorious fresh downland air. The view was splendid; the earth fresh and washed clean, the sky with just a hint of fleecy cloud speckling the blue. Over at The Gables their roof tiles had not completely dried yet, and the sun glinted and sparkled from droplets of water here and there, making the very prosaic school buildings glow like something from a fairy tale. It was, in short, good to be alive, and I fancy that I told myself just that and in no uncertain terms as I went about the business of preparing for the day. Indeed, I believe that I actually sang some rousing Gilbert and Sullivan air as I shaved and dressed, which was quite remarkable as being the first time for a good many months that I had felt so light-hearted.

I deeply regret to have to record that my agreeable mood received something of a setback when I clapped eyes on Holmes at breakfast. Martha had done us proud with the meal, and I like to think that I did what I could to cheer up my old friend, but it was all in vain. Holmes' sombre mood had returned with a vengeance, and he sat there, gloomily playing with his eggs and bacon, and occasionally muttering some reference to one or another of his old cases. Not his triumphs, though, not those cases which had made his name and his fortune, not the cases which had been reported in the national and international press; no, all he could hark back to now were the failures, few and far between though these had been, the cases where he had been unable to find missing gemstones, or a missing husband, the cases where the client had been in danger and Holmes had failed to spot it, with fatal results for the client. Dreary indeed were his ramblings, on that splendid sunny morning, which should have been all warmth and comfort.

As I have said, I tried to alter his mood, but all to no avail. So, when I had finished my own excellent meal, and offered Holmes my tobacco pouch – which he refused for about the first time ever since I had known him – I told him plainly, "Holmes, this is positively morbid. I don't know about you, but I'm off for a brisk walk, to take advantage of this unusually good weather. Will you not come with me, blow some of these cobwebs away?"

He lifted his head slowly, as if it were too heavy for him, gazed at me with dull eyes, waved a languid hand as if it caused him untold agonies to move it. "With your permission, Watson, I'll stay indoors. If the truth be told, I don't think I'm very good company at the moment. Oh, and don't be surprised if I don't appear at dinner, for I've no appetite just at the moment, and I prefer to think alone, in my room."

"Very well, Holmes, if you say so. But I think I'll be staying with you a week or so, if that will not inconvenience you?"

"As you wish, Doctor," he answered, without even looking at me.

I paused there only long enough to light my pipe, and then, considerably disgruntled, I set off for my walk. As I passed the kitchen door, old Martha appeared and put a hand on my arm. "Well, Doctor Watson?"

I shook my head. "The case is worse than I feared last night," I told her. "You did well to consult me, Martha. Never fear, though, we'll soon have him right as rain." And with that I left her, shaking her poor old head as she stared after me.

The doctor's sovereign anodyne, 'We'll soon have him right', but I asked myself as I went out on to the downs and sought the cliff path, how? How on earth was I to break through this barrier which Holmes had set up around himself, how was I to lift him from this slough of despond?

My pipe had gone out, as it will when you do not pay proper attention to filling it, when you are distracted and bothered by other things so that you do not pack it correctly. I teased the tobacco out, composed myself to doing it right this time, got a match lit and the tobacco bubbling nicely in the top of the bowl. That's better, I told myself. Take the job steadily, work out the proper approach, do it right. And just as with the humble briar, so too with Holmes. I needed a plan of campaign, needed to work out what must be done and tackle it in the right order.

First of all, I was still paying for that pony and trap, but it did not look as if I should need those again during my stay, so I might just as well return them to their owner in Brighton. I would take my lunch in the town, too, for I could not face Holmes until I had formulated some scheme that should wipe the frown from his brow and make him think that life was worth living.

My path led me once again past The Gables, where a couple of teams of energetic youths were just beginning a game of rugby. I had played myself in former days, and paused for a moment to watch. The master, a bright young fellow whom I knew slightly from my previous visits to Holmes, touched his cap and nodded a greeting.

"We've met before," I reminded him, "though I haven't been in these parts for some considerable time. Doctor John Watson, sir ..."

"Ah, of course, Mr Holmes' friend." He offered me his hand, but his brow clouded. "I trust you'll not take this amiss, Doctor, but here at The Gables some of us are just a touch concerned for Mr Holmes at the moment. He doesn't seem to get out and about as he once used to, and, to be plain, sir, the last time I spoke to him, he seemed ... well, distraught, to put it no higher."

I nodded. "Your concern does you credit, sir. I confess that I too am a touch bothered by Mr Holmes' mood of late. That is, in some sense, why I am here. I do not think it is anything of a serious nature that troubles him, I can find nothing organically wrong. But he is melancholy, there's no doubt of that, and I propose to stay until he is his old self. Never fear, we'll soon have him right."

And, feeling the most monstrous fraud that ever walked, I touched my hat and scurried off.

I retrieved my pony and trap from the little inn in Fulworth, and drove the short way into Brighton. I returned the pony and trap to the stable and settled the bill – as I think I told you, the distance to Holmes's little cottage was such that the walk was an easy one and a pleasant one, provided that this bright weather held. Only a sense of urgency had caused me to hire the trap on the previous evening. Urgency? And was there none now? Well, it is true that my innermost fears had not been realized, so that there was no longer any need for urgency in the sense of unseemly haste; but still I needed to work out what action I must take to save Holmes from his dejection. And quickly, for I knew only too well the destructive effect that boredom might have upon him. True, times had changed, and Holmes would no longer find it quite as easy to acquire those artificial stimulants that the supposedly staid and stuffy Victorian era had accepted without comment. But as a doctor I knew well enough that the legitimate sources of supply are not the only sources of supply. And these substances were perhaps the least troublesome of the alternatives that would face Holmes if he did not find something to occupy his mind, and soon.

Had he still been living in London, of course, I would immediately have prescribed a sea change. But he was here already, with all the fresh sea air, all the open country, that any man could wish for; and still he was unhappy. Perhaps, then, I should prescribe a return to London, I thought cynically.

It is perhaps fortunate that there were few visitors to the seaside at that time of year, for I stopped dead in my tracks. All my cynicism vanished, and I considered quite seriously the prospect of recommending to Holmes that he return to London, and indeed to work. But then I shook my head. After all, I had no idea just why Holmes had chosen to retire from practice whilst still comparatively youthful – he was even now little more than fifty. Holmes had never given any reason, and he was certainly not the sort of man who encourages idle chitchat on personal topics. Still, I could to some extent draw inferences from my own unhappy experiences over the weeks prior to my coming down here. My work was no longer satisfying or interesting, and I could well believe that a little place by the sea – a place not so very different from Holmes' cottage – would suit me down to the ground. But for how long? If that proverbial rose-covered cottage in its turn began to pall, then what was left? What, in a word, would jolt Holmes out of his dejected state, when work and holiday alike had lost their charm?

I shook my head sadly. It looked very much as if I should have to give the matter up as being beyond my poor wits to solve. After all, if Holmes himself could not arrive at any satisfactory answer, what was the probability that I could do so?

A moment ago, I said it was fortunate that there was nobody much about, so that I could stand there wool-gathering without interrupting the flow of pedestrians along the pavement. Yet even so early in the year the place was not entirely deserted, and indeed as I stood there I became aware that someone was standing at no great distance behind me. I moved aside slightly, lest I was indeed obstructing the path, and as I did so the man behind me spoke.

"Admiring the view? Or wondering where to take your luncheon?" The voice was a pleasant one, but the speaker was not English. The accent was strange, and yet somehow familiar.

I turned, ready to give this upstart a lesson in manners. "Really, sir, I don't see ..." and I stopped.

The man who had addressed me smiled, and removed his hat, so that I might see his face the better. I saw a man some thirty-five years of age, his dark hair thinning slightly at front so that his brow was impressive, that of a powerful thinker. He was somewhat under the average height, but with a gravity of deportment that made one look twice at him. The dark eyes, though, twinkled at me beneath the thick eyebrows, and beneath the heavy moustache lurked a smile. I looked at him, and looked again. Surely I knew him? I stared at him.

"Monsieur Sarkies?" I stammered. "Yes, it is ... Arshak Sarkies."

And Arshak Sarkies, for such indeed it was, smiled broadly and held out his hand to me.

At this point I must digress slightly. Those of you who were, in Kipling's memorable phrase, 'somewhere east of Suez' in the latter half of the nineteenth century may well need no introduction to the Sarkies brothers, but there are some to whom the name may not be immediately familiar, and for the benefit of these I had best explain matters here.

The family was, as you may possibly guess from the name, Armenian in origin, part of the most unheralded and yet arguably the greatest nation of merchants and traders that ever existed. There were four brothers, of whom the eldest, Martin, may be regarded as the founder of the family's fame and fortune. At one time an engineer, Martin Sarkies had turned his attention to the hotel business, and in a short while the phrase 'managed by the Sarkies brothers' became a guarantee of comfort and service. The brothers owned and managed a number of hotels at the time of which I write, but perhaps the most famous of them all was the 'Raffles' at Singapore, which had been in their care for around two decades, and was managed by another brother, Tigran.

Arshak Sarkies, who was now standing on the seafront at Brighton and shaking my hand vigorously, was the youngest of the four brothers. In addition to his professional and business reputation, he had another characteristic that had made his name a byword on the other side of the globe, namely his amazing generosity. Generous of purse to a fault – literally, for his liberality would later contribute to the firm's financial difficulties – he was also generous of spirit; in an age notable for its formality, even stiffness, he was almost universally known by his first name, and many a man who has run into a spot of business, or personal difficulty, has had good cause to be grateful to Arshak, who was never known to turn away a request for help.

I was one such man. It was many years ago, when I was out east, and there is no need to describe exactly what the trouble was – although I can say that it was my own foolish fault. But in my defence, I was young, and it was not a vicious or contemptible sort of fault I committed, and did nobody else any harm. Still, it was a nasty fix in which I found myself, and Arshak Sarkies helped me out of it, without fuss and with no sort of obligation expressed or implied. I owed him more than money could repay, and if I have seemed to sing his praises too loudly, you may think that there is good cause. I assure you, however, that I have, if anything, understated his greatness of heart.

Now, this is all very well, but you may be asking what this great-hearted hotelier from Singapore was doing in Brighton. It was, to be sure, the very first question that formed in my own mind, once I had properly taken in the simple fact of his being there. I knew that the brothers visited Europe frequently – indeed, Tigran, manager of the 'Raffles', would die in England a couple of years before the Great War, though of course we could not know that in 1905. But it was certainly odd to think that a man, whose home was basking in tropical heat, should seek out Brighton in late winter as a place to visit.

I stammered, "But ... but ... what ..."

Arshak Sarkies smiled at me, and waved a hand to indicate the hotels that stood round about us. "A professional visit, as one might say," he told me in a vague sort of fashion.

"What, you're not thinking of buying a hotel in Brighton, surely?"

"One must keep an eye open for business." The smile became enigmatic. "And another eye on one's competitors. But you, Doctor Watson? You are perhaps permitting yourself a break from your practice, a well-earned rest, a quiet few days in this quiet season?"

I told him, "In a sense, it is a professional matter which brings me here."

"Ah, you frown, old friend. Can I help?"

"You are too kind, as always," I said, "but I fear that it is a purely medical matter. Another old friend, Mr Sherlock Holmes ..."

"Mr Holmes? Is he here, too, then? But, you said it was a medical matter? Is Mr Holmes unwell?"

"You cannot possibly know Holmes, Arshak. Even you, with your vast acquaintance ..."

He waved a hand. "I cannot claim that honour. But I assure you that I have followed Mr Holmes' career, as illustrated by your own brilliant accounts, with the keenest possible interest. And I should esteem it a favour if you could introduce me to him ... unless, that is, the matter is very grave?" And he regarded me anxiously.

"Oh, it's nothing physical, I'm sure of that. It is just ... well, in a lesser man than Holmes, I'd have called it boredom."

"Ah! *Ennui?*"

"Just so."

"Tedium?"

"Indeed."

"*Le cafard?*"

27

"The point has been made, Arshak."

He laughed aloud at my starchiness. "Let me buy you some luncheon, my friend ..."

"Not a bit of it," I told him. "I shall buy you luncheon, as some small recompense for all that I owe you." I glanced at my watch. "It is still a little early, though, so perhaps an aperitif first?"

"Indeed." He sighed. "Though I could wish that your English barmen might learn to make a decent cocktail. I assure you, old friend, at the 'Raffles' we have a man who is a positive genius with gin.[1] As it is, I shall be obliged to settle for what your music-hall song calls, dismally and accurately, 'a half of half-and-half '."[2]

"Oh, we can do better than that!" I said, and we went off arm in arm to find some refreshment.

Over luncheon, Arshak asked me more about Holmes, and the dark cloud that had descended upon my old friend. I told him some of the details, and digressed as far as saying that at the moment I could sympathize with Holmes, for my own work seemed no longer to hold the attraction that once it held.

And Arshak sat there listening intently, like any Harley Street specialist. When I had done, he shrugged, and said, "Well, Watson, but it seems to me that the answer is clear.

---

[1] It is almost certainly Ngiam Tong Boon, the inventor of the legendary Singapore Sling, or Gin Sling, who is meant here. The precise date of the drink's creation is a bigger mystery than the date of the Pyramids; some authorities suggest as late as 1915, but some claim it was available to thirsty travellers a decade earlier. It should be noted that Dr Watson's memory is often unreliable, so this conversation should not be quoted as a source in any debate on this topic!

[2] 'Half-and-half' for those youngsters who do not know, is – or was – a mixture of mild and bitter beer in equal measures.

You need a holiday, and what's more Mr Sherlock Holmes needs a holiday."

With a touch of exasperation, I replied, "But have I not just told you? That is the crux of the whole matter. His life at the moment is one long holiday, and thus the relish has gone from everything he does."

Arshak shrugged again. "Oh, I did not mean that he should move here to Brighton for a week. No, I had a very different location in mind. A complete change of scenery, in fact. For both of you."

"Where, then?"

"Singapore. The Raffles Hotel, in fact."

"You are joking!"

"Not a bit of it."

"But ..." And I stared at him. "You are really not joking?"

He shook his head. "Not in the least." He smiled at my confusion. "People do come to the 'Raffles' for a holiday, you know."

"Yes, I know that. But ..." and I shook my head.

"What is your objection, then?"

"Well, the distance, the time to get there ..."

Arshak shook his head. "A couple of weeks only. No longer than it took me to get to England. A pleasant sea voyage, the captain's table, the company of beautiful women and congenial men, good food and wine. Why, the journey is a holiday in itself. I return next week, as a matter of fact. Will you not come with me?"

"I would, like a shot. If it were only me ... but, I couldn't leave Holmes."

"And why leave him? The whole object of the exercise is to take him along. You will both be my guests, of course. Why should Mr Holmes not come along?"

"I can't give you any coherent reason why not, and I'm sure Holmes himself could not give you any coherent reason why not."

"Well, then?"

"But I'm equally sure that Holmes would never agree to go."

"H'mm." Arshak sat there, drumming his fingers on the tabletop. Then his face lit up. "Tell me, Watson, did you not once quote Mr Holmes as saying something like, 'My mind rebels at stagnation ... give me an abstruse cryptogram, the most knotty of problems, and I am in my element'?"

"Very likely," I said gloomily. "It's exactly the sort of nonsense Holmes would spout."

"But is it true?"

"Oh, I suppose it's true enough, as far as it goes. Certainly Holmes thrives on activity, which is half ... more than half ... the present trouble."

"In that case," said Arshak, "we shall have him. Just introduce me to Mr Holmes, old friend, and leave the rest to me."

Arshak had a carriage at his disposal, and we took the short drive into Fulworth, where I believe my old friend caused quite a stir, judging by the frenzied twitching of lace curtains as we strolled down the narrow, steep little street that was all the place boasted. Then we took the cliff path – a very different walk from that of the previous evening, I reflected. I told Arshak of my summons and my soaking, and we laughed over it together.

Holmes was moping in his room when we reached his cottage, and Martha had to call him. He looked quizzically as he saw Arshak standing there.

"Ah, Holmes, may I introduce Arshak Sarkies, from the famous hotel dynasty? You've heard me speak of him, I know, and if by some chance you haven't, then at any rate you'll have heard of the famous Raffles Hotel."

"Your name is familiar to me, Mr Sarkies," said Holmes, "and I am delighted to meet you."

"And I to meet you at last, sir, for your name is at least as familiar to me as mine is to you." Arshak looked at my friend in admiration. "It was indeed a sad loss to society when you elected to retire from practice, Mr Holmes." He shook his head. "In fact, I wish you were in Singapore right this moment, or that I might persuade you to return there with me next week."

Despite himself, Holmes was intrigued, as he was by any little puzzle. "Oh, and why is that?" he asked.

Arshak shrugged. "You see, Mr Holmes, we have … ah, a little problem at the Raffles Hotel. Oh, it is nothing serious, nothing that will harm our guests, or put them off staying, but still … there is no point discussing it, for you are not there, and there's an end of it." And he changed the subject, completely ignoring all Holmes' efforts to define or discuss the 'little problem'.

At a convenient break in the conversation, I interjected, "You know, Holmes, I haven't been anywhere near Singapore for years, now. I wouldn't mind going to the 'Raffles' and have a look at the place, for I've heard so much about it. And if you went along too, you could look into Arshak's problem."

Holmes waved a languid hand, in the manner of some effeminate Roman emperor ordering up another dozen Christians for the arena, and mumbled some nonsense or other.

"Why not?" asked Arshak eagerly. "The management of the 'Raffles' would pay your expenses, of course, and a reasonable fee for your services. Can I not tempt you out of retirement for this one last case, Mr Holmes?"

I added my voice to that of the tempter. "Yes, Holmes, why not?"

Holmes looked from one to another of us. "You think I might be of some use?" he asked Arshak.

"There is truly no-one I would rather see at the Raffles Hotel than you, Mr Holmes."

Holmes smiled. "I feel that I am the victim of a conspiracy," he told us. "But it is, I know, a benign and friendly conspiracy." He stood up and offered Arshak his hand. "Very well, Mr Sarkies, you have intrigued me, and made me a very kind offer, which it would be churlish to refuse. I am your man. I shall come with you to the Raffles Hotel."

"I am delighted to hear you say so, Mr Holmes. And now, I fear I must take my leave."

"I'll go with you as far as the village," I told him.

As I accompanied Arshak down the cliff path back into Fulworth, I asked him, "But what will you say when we get to Singapore and Holmes asks the nature of your problem?"

"Oh, we have a problem, right enough," said Arshak very seriously. "It concerns the veranda."

I laughed. "Oh? A loose board, perhaps?"

"More important than that. We get wild animals lurking round the place."

"Wild animals?"

"Singapore is not quite so settled as London or Brighton, you know. We sometimes get animals visiting the hotel. Indeed, some of the sporting guests sit up at night on the veranda in a wicker chair, with a gun, to see what arrives. A pig, a large snake, once a tiger … though I believe it was only a small tiger."

"That sounds like fun. I might sit up myself a night or two."

32

"I shall lend you the wicker chair and the gun."

I stopped, put a hand on his arm. "But, Arshak, though I'm sure it bothers some of your more nervous guests, it is hardly the sort of thing that Mr Holmes can help you with!"

"And did I say it was? I said I should like to see him at the 'Raffles', and so I should, for it will cheer him up. And I said we had a slight problem, and so we have. If he chose to infer some connection between two unrelated statements of fact, that is hardly my fault."

I laughed. "You should have been a diplomat."

"And what do you think the owner, or manager, of a large hotel is, then?"

* * *

One of the many difficulties the writer must face is that of what to omit. The sea voyage from England to Singapore would probably furnish material for a dozen books of travel, adventure and romance – and for all I know, it has done so. But for all the relevance it has to my present tale, it was of no greater significance than a second-class return from Baker Street to Uxbridge in the rush hour; and I shall pass over it in these few paragraphs accordingly.

There were, for me at least, only two points of interest connected with the voyage. The first was that Holmes, to my immense relief, began at last to come out from beneath the dark cloud which had hung over him. A day or so after we had left England, he emerged from his cabin and began to take an interest in our fellow passengers. Too much of an interest for comfort, as far as some of them would have been concerned, had they known that they were under his keen eye, for he soon started to mutter things like, 'The Russian count over there is actually a card-sharper from Lancashire', or 'That lady is most definitely not the wife of the man with whom she is travelling'. He would throw out these snippets of information in the most casual way, then give a sidelong glance at his listeners, inviting queries and praise for all the world like some debutante inviting compliments and proposals of marriage. I myself was hardened to this behaviour, and would have left him to stew in his own juice; but to Arshak this was all very new and very exciting, and he played up to Holmes magnificently, with 'But how ... ?' and 'Why ... ?' and 'Marvellous!' and the like. So all in all, Holmes was very soon pretty much his old self.

Which, of course, brings me to the second significant point. As Holmes' old powers of observation and deduction returned to the full – to say nothing of his acid wit – I began to fear more and more how he would react when he realized the deception, uncovered the truth, knew the trick that Arshak and I were playing on him. I was sure that Holmes would either turn round and get the first boat back to England, or sink back into that despondency from which he had just emerged.

The day before we were due to dock in Singapore, I took Arshak aside and told him of my concerns. He listened carefully, then waved my fears aside, saying, "But it is too late, my friend, we are almost there. What, realistically, can Mr Holmes do now, be he ever so angry with us?"

"Well ..."

"At the very worst, he will return home, and will thus have another restful sea voyage. Why, you have remarked yourself upon how much better he has been these past few days."

"Well, that's true, I suppose," I said doubtfully.

"And if Mr Holmes is the man I think him to be, he will laugh heartily at the whole thing, and settle down for a few weeks rest at the Raffles Hotel. And never fear, we shall look after him ... and you."

We duly arrived, and docked. As we set off ashore, Arshak paused at the top of the gangplank, pointed, and told me, "There is my brother, Tigran. He has evidently come to welcome me home, and I know that he will be delighted to have two such distinguished guests."

I looked, to get my first glimpse of Tigran Sarkies, manager of the fabled Raffles Hotel. He was a couple of years older than Arshak, and a little thinner, his clean-shaven face a contrast to Arshak's luxuriant moustache, but the family resemblance was evident. Tigran was meticulously dressed, and wore a pair of gold-rimmed spectacles – I would later learn that he had something of a reputation as a dandy. Just now, though, there was a worried look on his face, and Arshak too remarked upon this fact.

"H'mm," said he, "Tigran does not seem quite as pleased to see his brother as one might have hoped. I trust there is nothing amiss at the 'Raffles'," he added anxiously.

We reached dry land, passed quickly through the usual formalities, and sought out Tigran Sarkies.

As we approached, he rushed forward and shook Arshak warmly by the hand.

"Never was I more delighted to see you, brother," he told him.

"I must say, you don't look it."

Tigran frowned. "Oh, there is terrible news, dreadful news. But now you are here, I feel much better."

"Tigran, may I introduce two guests for the 'Raffles'? This is Doctor John Watson, an old friend of mine ..."

"Delighted, delighted," said Tigran absently.

" ... and this is Mr Sherlock Holmes."

"What! That is to say, not ... not Mr Sherlock Holmes of Baker Street, the famous detective?"

"None other," said Arshak calmly.

"Although I have left Baker Street, and ... except for the occasional foray into the criminal underworld ... left practice as well," added Holmes.

Tigran put a hand to his brow. "But ... but this is wonderful news. But how on earth did you know, brother Arshak? It is true that I thought to telegraph, to see if I could not contact you on the boat, but I decided against it. And then you must have set off ... when? Two weeks ago? Three? How did you know to bring Mr Holmes, so long before it happened?"

"Before what happened?" we all three dutifully chorused.

"What are you talking about, brother? What is the matter?" added Arshak.

Tigran removed his spectacles, and polished them carefully on a silk handkerchief. "Why," said he, "since it only happened yesterday, and the news cannot possibly have reached you, how did you know we should need Mr Holmes' services? How on earth did you know about the murder?"

Chapter Three

The Background to the Case

Holmes, of course, was in his natural element now. "Murder? Who? When? How?" came out all at once, causing the unfortunate Tigran Sarkies to step back quickly.

Arshak interrupted, "Not at the 'Raffles' itself, surely?"

"No, thank Heaven," replied Tigran, recovering his composure somewhat. "But it involves one of our former residents, Mr Derek Masterton ... you know him, Arshak."

Arshak's face fell. "Of course. But I trust that he has ..."

"No, no."

"Then how is he concerned?"

"It is his wife's sister who has been killed ... poisoned."

"Good Lord!" Arshak frowned. "Though I cannot recall that I have ever met Mrs Masterton's sister in person."

Tigran shook his head. "I do not think she had been here to Singapore previously, and certainly I had never met her until just the other day. No, she arrived here from London only recently with her husband, a Mr Charles Gerard. It is Mr Gerard who has been arrested for the murder, and I must say that things look very bad against him."

"You sum things up admirably," Holmes added. "But then if the matter is so cut-and-dried, what would you have me do?"

"Well, look into it, make sure that Superintendent Ingham ... he is our local police chief, you know ... has the right of it," replied Tigran. "If so, then all well and good, but if not, then we must catch the real murderer. Mrs Masterton is, as you may imagine, quite distraught over her sister's death, and I would wish to give her at least the consolation of knowing that every effort is being made to avenge her dreadful murder." He permitted himself a bleak smile. "But I am forgetting myself entirely, thanks to this terrible business. You must forgive me, gentlemen. Come along to the hotel, and we shall make you comfortable."

Holmes seemed about to demur at this and insist upon starting work at once, but the rest of us pointed out the sense of our getting settled in, disposing of our luggage, getting our bearings in these new surroundings, and what have you, and he reluctantly allowed himself to be persuaded.

From the Tanjong Pagar wharf, where we had disembarked, it is no great distance at all to the Raffles Hotel. We bowled along in Tigran's smart carriage, and now, for about the first time, the magnitude of the contrast with old England hit me. True, there had been a lengthy sea voyage that had to some extent got us accustomed to the heat; but there had been sea breezes to cool things down slightly. Here, the heat seemed a solid wall, almost a living thing which grabbed you by the throat. And then, too, life at sea had been a calm and leisurely sort of thing, not at all like the hustle and bustle that now assailed our eyes and – more to the point – our ears.

I sat back, fanning my face with my hat, and fairly gawped at the activity around us. The sea and seafront seemed black with vessels of all shapes and sizes. Here were passenger ships tying up at the wharves, there were merchantmen with every cargo imaginable, and so on down to the tiny rowing boats that ferried passengers and goods from great liners moored further out in deep water. As you may imagine, with all this shipping loading or unloading, the land too was not entirely devoid of a certain amount of hustle and bustle. In fact, the carriage was obliged to stop more than once as the way was so crowded with all sorts of vehicles, and all manner of men, representing, as it seemed to me, every race under the blazing sun.

I had scarcely had time to take a proper look about me, when Arshak touched my arm and nodded ahead of us. "Behold," said he with a pardonable touch of drama, "the Raffles Hotel."

I turned my head, looked when he indicated, and gave an involuntary gasp of surprise. I had heard of the 'Raffles', of course – and who has not? – but never actually seen it, and it was somewhat different from what I had imagined. Not unduly high, perhaps, a couple of storeys only, but it seemed to cover an enormous acreage of ground. White, cool, airy, spacious – it seemed a veritable oasis of calm and comfort, even from the outside.

"It is indeed impressive," I told Arshak.

"But just wait until you see the interior. I imagine you will be glad to get inside, out of the heat?"

"Oh, the heat doesn't bother me," I told him. "Quite like old times, in fact. Does the heat trouble you, Holmes?"

"The heat?" Holmes stared at me as if he had not heard me. "I had not noticed it, Watson." And he went back to his own thoughts, impervious alike to heat or cold, unconscious of the busy swarms of folk on land and sea, quite self-contained, his mind completely occupied by the problem that faced him, so that Tigran had to nudge him gently when we came to a halt before the entrance.

Arshak showed Holmes and me to a couple of comfortable rooms. Although it is true that the heat did not trouble me overly, none the less I should have been grateful for the chance of a short rest, but Holmes was clearly in no mood for idleness. His room was across the corridor from my own, and through the door, which he had not bothered to shut properly, I saw him fling his bags onto the bed in a careless fashion that would have broken the heart of the poor little chambermaid who had tidied up the room earlier that morning. Without even a glance round at the interior of the room, he turned on his heel and hurried across to my door, rubbing his hands as he did so. "Still unpacking, Watson? Come along, my dear fellow, we have no time to waste. We can settle in later, when all is resolved." And off he went along the corridor, seeking out Tigran Sarkies for more details of the case.

Arshak, who had just shown me to my room and was standing by the door, raised an eyebrow. "Mr Holmes' enthusiasm is admirable," said he.

"Oh, indeed it is. But it can be a touch wearing at times." And I resigned myself to leaving my own humble arrangements until later, and Arshak and I followed Holmes to Tigran's private office, where Arshak tapped on the door and looked in.

"Ah, come in and sit down." Tigran waved us to chairs, and offered his gold cigarette case.

Holmes produced his ancient briar pipe. "Does anyone object?"

I glanced hastily round, and was relieved to see that the windows were open, and that an electric fan turned lazily above our heads.

Holmes was saying, "The more details you can give me at this stage, Mr Sarkies, the easier will be my task later, so pray tell me everything you know, and with your permission I shall ask any questions as they occur to me."

"Of course. Although I know little more than I have already told you." Tigran removed his spectacles and polished them, as if arranging his thoughts in their proper order. "Very well. As I have said, my own interest in the case arises solely from the fact that Mr Derek Masterton was for a long time a resident here at the 'Raffles' ..."

Holmes raised a hand. "Forgive me, resident rather than guest?"

Tigran inclined his head. "We draw a distinction between visitors, those guests who honour us only temporarily, and the residents who make the 'Raffles' more or less their permanent home during their time in Singapore. For the single men particularly ... and there are lots of single men here, for the place is still somewhat of a frontier town, despite recent tremendous advances ... here at the 'Raffles' we offer all the comforts of home with none of the worries, and that arrangement is highly agreeable to many of them."

"I understand perfectly." Holmes smiled. "Indeed, were I here permanently, I have no doubt that I should be a resident here myself. Please continue."

"Mr Masterton has his own export agency," Tigran went on, "and handles a variety of local goods, as I understand it. He first arrived here in Singapore, and at the 'Raffles', some

41

four or five years ago, and took rooms here on a more or less permanent basis. I ... and Arshak here ... got to know him quite well. A couple of years go, Mr Masterton visited England, and whilst there he met and married a Miss Anya Cardell. They returned here as man and wife, and for a time they resided here in Mr Masterton's old rooms." Tigran smiled. "I honestly believe that Mr Masterton would have stayed here indefinitely, but the new Mrs Masterton was naturally anxious to become mistress of her own domain, and soon after their return they secured a very pleasant house in the town, no great distance away. They now have two small children, so their decision to move out of the hotel was probably a wise one." He smiled. "Despite their desertion of the 'Raffles' we all remained friends, and it is for the sake of that friendship that I would wish to assist the family in any way possible."

"I understand," said Holmes. "And then, if I read it aright, Mrs Masterton's sister has also married recently, her husband being this Mr Charles Gerard, and the young couple came here to visit their relatives, the Mastertons?"

Tigran nodded. "As Arshak here said, we had no idea as to what other family the Mastertons might have, for they never mentioned the subject. Then, last week, Mr Masterton told me that his wife's sister and her new husband ... they had been married only the week before they left England ... were arriving shortly. I asked, naturally, if they would be staying with the Mastertons, or if perhaps they would honour the 'Raffles' for the duration of their visit. Mr Masterton told me, with some embarrassment, that they would not be staying with him, nor yet here at the hotel, but that he ... Mr Masterton himself ... had found accommodation for them on the other side of the town."

"Oh?"

The usually urbane Tigran shrugged his shoulders, and looked down at the blotter on his desk.

"Mr Sarkies? Did you not find it rather odd that the Masterton family should not invite the newcomers, or, failing that, that they should not stay here, where Mr Masterton had been so happy?"

"Well, then, Mr Holmes, regarding the Raffles Hotel itself, as far as I could make it out, the young couple had not very much money. We pride ourselves on our reasonable rates, of course," he added, "but even so they wanted something a little … ah, cheaper. They were, as I understand it, lodged in a rooming house." And he shrugged his elegant shoulders once again, as if to reinforce the fact that it was no fault of his. "As to their not staying with the Mastertons … well, no doubt they had their reasons, and it was scarcely for me to enquire into them."

"Indeed not. But you must have had some thoughts on the matter? Did you not suspect any family quarrel, some rift between the sisters, shall we say? Odd, surely, that Mrs Masterton should never mention the fact that she had a sister?"

"I had no idea of any such thing," said Tigran rather abruptly, as if he wished to close the subject. "The only reason that I could see was that apparently Mr Charles Gerard was of an independent turn of mind, and did not wish to be further beholden to his brother-in-law, Mr Masterton."

"Further beholden, you say?"

"I gather that Mr Gerard had hopes that Mr Masterton would offer him some employment, and thus secure him a competence, enable the young couple to transfer to more salubrious surroundings, move up in the world, so to speak."

"I see. And did Mr Masterton happen to indicate ..."

Tigran raised a hand. "You understand, Mr Holmes, in my profession one does not pry into the private affairs of one's guests?" He smiled. "Indeed, one spends a good deal of one's time trying to forget little pieces of information which one has inadvertently come across."

Holmes laughed. "Of course. And the Gerards arrived a few days go?"

Tigran thought for a moment. "Today is Friday, and they arrived on Monday."

"And poor Mrs Gerard was murdered yesterday, that is, Thursday?"

Tigran nodded. "She had thus been here a mere four days by the calendar ... two full days only, if we discount the day of her arrival and that of her murder." He looked keenly at Holmes. "Hardly long enough to make enemies here in Singapore."

"No, indeed not. And the police evidently share that view, for you say they have arrested Mr Gerard?"

"That is so," said Tigran. "And I must say that there is other evidence beyond the purely circumstantial, and it seems very damning. It appears that Mr Gerard purchased for his wife a box of sweetmeats. The climate here is not conducive to the storage of chocolate, you know, and there is a little firm in the town which makes a speciality, 'Singapore Sugarplums', which consist of a hard sugar-candy outside, with a variety of fillings, some soft, some hard, some liquid, as I understand, though I do not much eat them myself. It appears that some of these sweetmeats contained arsenic."

Arshak gasped, Holmes nodded, and I muttered to myself, too low to be audible, "The old poisoned chocolate ploy, once more?"

Holmes, who has acute hearing, gave me a glance. "As Watson here so accurately says, it is a very hackneyed device," he told Tigran.

"To be sure," replied Tigran, "but effective."

"H'mm. But if Mr Gerard is the perpetrator, he has been less than effective in hiding his crime?" Holmes shook his head. "And then, what motive would he have ... especially when one considers ... no!" He shook his head again, then rose to his feet. "Well, Mr Sarkies, you have admirably summarized the obvious facts for me. I wonder, is it possible to talk to Mrs Masterton? Is she at her home?"

"She is," said Tigran, "but she is much upset by this sad affair, as you will appreciate. Mr Masterton informs me that the doctor has given her a strong sedative, and she has not emerged from her own room as yet."

"And Mr Masterton himself? Where is he?"

"He is with his wife, of course. I may add that he, too, is much unsettled by this dreadful affair."

"I see. And the police officer in charge of the case ... a Superintendent Ingham, I think you said?"

"Yes, you will find him at the police station. Arshak here will show you the way."

* * *

"I have heard of you, of course, Mr Holmes." Superintendent Ingham was a tall, solidly built man with a face burned brick red by the sun. He smiled at Holmes, and held out his hand. He waved us to chairs, and I was glad to see the little electric fan on his desk was full on. I moved my chair surreptitiously, to take advantage of the slight breeze it afforded. Ingham was saying, "And I'd esteem it an honour to work with you, sir, on any other case than this. Frankly, the matter seems open and shut, with little scope for the exercise of your talents."

"So I understand. But you do not object if I ask one or two questions myself?"

"Go ahead, sir."

"Mr Gerard is in custody here?"

The Superintendent nodded. "I have him in the cells, sir. Did you want to talk to him?"

"He denies it, of course?"

"Of course." Ingham laughed, and then grew sober. "I must say that he does a very good job of pretending innocence."

"But you yourself have no doubts on the matter?"

Ingham shook his head. "As far as I can make out … and this is on Gerard's own testimony … they knew nobody here in Singapore, with the exception of her sister, Mrs Masterton, and I don't think she's a suspect, do you? And then Gerard undoubtedly took the poisoned sweets to his wife, according to the landlady of the rooming house, who has no good reason to lie." He shrugged and looked at his desk. "And then the landlady adds that the couple quarrelled, a heated quarrel, the day before the poor lady died. Pretty open-and-shut, I think. Have you any doubts?"

"Oh, I cannot say at this early stage. I am just a little curious as to certain points, that is all. The landlady did not happen to overhear the cause of this quarrel at all?"

"I'm afraid not. But the cause hardly seems relevant." Ingham looked at Holmes. "You're still unconvinced, I see? Yes? So you'll talk to Gerard? I was going to question him myself anyway, and together we may get the facts from him."

46

"I should prefer to see these peculiar sugarplums which are at the root of the problem, before I speak to Mr Gerard."

"As you wish. They are in our little laboratory here. I'll take you, Gerard will keep for a while."

The Superintendent led us down corridors and up stairs, finally opening a door that led to a small but well-equipped chemical laboratory. "This is Doctor Oong," said Ingham. "Doctor, a colleague, Doctor John Watson, and the famous Mr Sherlock Holmes."

Dr Oong, a cheerful Chinese gentleman, beamed happily at us. "Delighted, delighted! Even here, Mr Holmes, we know your name and your work. I take it that it is the poisoning which brings you here, rather than a social call?"

"I confess that I am intrigued by these 'Singapore Sugarplums'," said Holmes.

"Ah, yes." Dr Oong indicated three or four boxes that lay on a bench. "Take a look, Doctor Watson, and you, Mr Holmes. Those boxes," and he pointed, "were bought by my assistant, for the purposes of experimentation. That one is ... ah, just a little bit more sinister. Look at the genuine article first, though."

I picked up one of the boxes he had indicated as being harmless. The lid was printed in bright colours, with a view of Singapore in the centre, and various dragons and other auspicious and mythical beasts lurking in the corners. It bore the legend, 'Singapore Sugarplums, the Old, Original, and BEST!' and in smaller letters beneath, 'Singapore Sugarplum Manuf. Coy., (Pty.), Singapore', and then a florid and illegible signature and a couple of Chinese characters, and finally, 'None genuine without this signature and seal. ACCEPT NO WORTHLESS IMITATIONS'.

"H'mm." I opened the box. Within were ranged exactly twenty-four sugar-coated confections, all much of a size, but with variations as to shape and colour, some being round, some square, some oval, some diamond shaped; while as to hue, there were palest pastels alongside some very garish tones. I could see that there were six different centres – the inside of the lid bore a key to aid in the identification of these – with four examples of each nestling in the box.

I tapped the hard outside of one of the sweets. "Just sugar?" I asked Dr Oong.

He nodded. "Sugar and water, with a little gum and starch, and various colouring and flavouring materials." He picked up another box and produced one of the confections. He rummaged in a pocket and took out a tiny penknife with a mother-of-pearl handle. "You see?" And before I had properly grasped what he intended, he had levered an irregularly shaped section of the coating from the base of the sweet, to reveal a white centre. "A child could do it. Would you care to try, Doctor Watson?"

"Indeed I should." I used my own penknife, and made a pretty fair hash of the first one or two attempts; but with practice I found that I could remove a tolerably regular disc from the base without damaging the rest of the sweet too much. "And for re-fixing it? Sugar and water?"

Dr Oong nodded. "That, or ordinary gum. These confections are very sweet to the taste, and that would mask any foreign materials."

"And I suppose the same goes for the taste of the arsenic? I asked.

Dr Oong nodded. He indicated a little dish, upon which rested four of the sweets, each with a little paper label, marked, 'A', 'B', 'C', and 'D'.

"Two of these are untouched, and two have been tampered with by me and my assistants," he said. "Would you care to identify which are which?"

I took a close look at each of the four in turn. It was no easy task, but I fancied that two bore some slight traces of having been tinkered with. "'A' and 'C' are innocuous," I told Dr Oong, "but 'B' and 'D' are not."

He smiled at me. "It is perhaps fortunate that we did not make the experiment in earnest, Doctor," he told me. "'A' is indeed original and untouched, but 'C' is one which I have ... if you will forgive the pun ... doctored. Though not, of course, with real arsenic," he added, as I hastily dropped 'C' back on the dish.

"Good Lord! Well, I couldn't have said which was which, not accurately. And the repairs are just sugar syrup?"

Dr Oong nodded. "Sugar syrup in one case, a colourless gum in the other."

Holmes added, "I see that four of the sweets are missing from the offending box. What quantity of arsenic would they represent?"

Dr Oong frowned. "Now, that is the curious thing, Mr Holmes. It is true that I found arsenic in some of the other sweets in the box, but not all."

Holmes raised an eyebrow. "Oh?"

Dr Oong picked up the box that he had earlier pointed out as containing the poisoned sweets and showed it to us. Four of the spaces were empty, and the other sweets all showed signs of having been examined by the police doctor, for the shells were all split and crushed where samples had been scooped out, taken for analysis. "You are right, Mr Holmes, to say that four are missing altogether. That is as we found the box, the others were originally found untouched but have, of course, been carefully examined here. Now, you will observe that the four sweets which are missing are all the same variety of centre, namely 'Walnut Whirls'?"

We nodded.

"Very well," said Dr Oong, "in the stomach of poor Mrs Gerard, I found traces of the 'Walnut Whirls', and a sufficient quantity of arsenic to kill her twice over. On examining the other sweets in the box, I found arsenic in only four, the 'Violet Cremes', and in the same sort of quantity, that is to say, two of the sweets would represent a lethal dose for an average adult person."

"So four would certainly do the trick? Yes, I see." Holmes frowned. "But what of the other centres in the poisoned box?"

Dr Oong shook his head. "Perfectly harmless."

I put a hand to my head. "But do you seriously tell me that only eight of the twenty-four sweets contained poison?"

Dr Oong nodded. "So it would appear. I can speak definitely as to the four 'Violet Cremes', and I assume the 'Walnut Whirls' were similarly adulterated."

I went on, "So if someone should eat the rest? They would be unharmed?"

"Perfectly unharmed," said Dr Oong. "Eight sweets were deadly poisonous, the rest perfectly innocuous." He took one of the sorry-looking shells from the box. "Would you care to try the remains of a 'Caramel Cube', Doctor Watson?"

"Not in a thousand years! But ... you do see what this means, Holmes?"

Holmes nodded. "It means a very detailed knowledge of the tastes and preferences of the person for whom the sweets were intended." He sighed. "And that, I'm afraid, means that things look very bad indeed for Mr Gerard."

Chapter Four

The Testimony of Charles Gerard

Superintendent Ingham slapped Holmes on the back in a kindly fashion. "Did you really think you could find anything that might clear Mr Gerard, then?"

"Oh, I did not intend any sort of reflection upon your deductive powers," said Holmes with a smile, as Superintendent Ingham thanked Dr Oong, and then led us back along the maze of corridors. "However, I am sure you will agree that there are puzzling aspects to the case?"

Superintendent Ingham paused at the door of his own room, stood aside to let us enter, and told us to sit down. Then he took out his pipe, examined it and lit it, and then he frowned. "Puzzling aspects, Mr Holmes? Such as?"

"Such as, why, if Mr Gerard wished to kill Mrs Gerard, after only a couple of months of marriage, as I understand it ..."

Here the Superintendent nodded. "Mr Gerard confirmed that, showed me the certificate, all above board." His lip curled ever so slightly. "He seemed ... seemed, I say ... to take it hard that Mrs Gerard should die after so short a time. Still, it wouldn't be the first time that a man killed his wife after a very short time would it, Doctor?" he appealed to me.

"Wouldn't, I'm afraid. Seen it myself often enough, and so has Holmes here."

Ingham nodded, and said, "I'm sure we've all seen it, more's the pity. But I'm interrupting you, Mr Holmes. Please go on."

"Whether his grief is real or bogus, is it not very odd that he should kill his wife here, where her sister and brother-in-law would be sure to take notice, to make a fuss, to demand justice, rather than kill her in England? Unless there are other relatives back there?" And he looked at Ingham.

The Superintendent shook his head. "Now you mention it, I happen to know that Mrs Masterton had no family apart from her sister, because she himself told me as much. I know the two of them quite well," he added parenthetically, "for Derek Masterton and I belong to the same club, drink at the same bar at the 'Raffles', and what have you. We're a close-knit little community here in many ways, so that's not so odd. H'mm! What *is* odd is just what you've said, Mr Holmes. Yes, why would he wait until he was here, where her sister was sure to make a fuss, instead of doing the job in London, where there was nobody much to miss her?"

"Or again," said Holmes, "they had just disembarked from a lengthy sea voyage. Why did Gerard not simply wait until dark, take his wife on deck for a romantic stroll, and simply push her overboard?"

"Really, Holmes!" I said.

"It has been done before," he pointed out.

"Perhaps he only just decided ..." I began, then broke off. "No, that won't do! Arsenic implies premeditation."

Holmes nodded. "And it surely implies also that Mr Gerard ... if he is indeed the murderer ... had planned the murder as long ago as several weeks? He cannot have dared to rely upon finding a supply of arsenic here in Singapore, where he did not know his way around the place, and much less could he know the local rules and regulations."

I nodded in my turn – I should perhaps digress here to remind you that back in 1905 the regulations concerning poisons were by no means as rigid as they later became. Anyone who looked respectable could obtain arsenic in England simply by signing the poison register at any pharmacy – and they would not be asked to provide any evidence that the name with which they had signed was their own. All very lax, and all very regrettable, I know, and a good many murders were committed as a result, until the thing became a national scandal and the rules were tightened up. But such was the state of affairs at the time of which I write. Still, as Holmes said, a stranger in a strange land would not be able to rely upon similar laxity on the part of the local authorities. If Charles Gerard had poisoned his wife with arsenic, it was logical to suppose that he had bought it in England, before ever he left. I shuddered at the thought. "Horrid, Holmes!"

Holmes waved this sentimental nonsense aside. "So, we are to suppose that Mr Gerard is a hardened and heartless plotter who intended to kill his wife almost from the very wedding day, who bought arsenic in London soon after his marriage, but who then entirely failed to use it until he had arrived at a place where its use would surely draw attention to him and would be certain to land him in prison? No, my dear Ingham, it makes no sense at all."

The Superintendent frowned. "You make out a convincing enough case, Mr Holmes, I must admit. But then, if Mr Gerard did not poison his wife, who on earth did? It surely cannot have been her own sister? And nobody else knew her in Singapore, as far as we are aware."

"But you are not sure?"

Superintendent Ingham shook his head. "The murder was only committed yesterday, sir. There has been no time to look into the matter fully." He smiled at Holmes. "But it seems clear that we must make a start. I propose to begin by talking to Mr Gerard himself and getting his side of the story."

"You said, I think, that you had not yet properly questioned him?" said Holmes.

"Not yet, no. He seemed much too upset. Or perhaps he genuinely was upset," added Ingham thoughtfully. "In any event, I said that I must arrest him for the murder of his wife, and asked what he had to tell me. He denied killing Mrs Gerard, and then he more or less collapsed in tears. I had him locked up downstairs, and that's where he has been ever since."

"Tell me," said Holmes, "did you, or he, mention the poisoned candies?"

Ingham shook his head. "I took them from the room, thinking it likely that they were the source of the poison, the cause of death. But I haven't told Gerard the results of the analysis." He smiled a grim smile again. "I reckoned that if he had poisoned them, he wouldn't need me to tell him that they had poison in them. While if he had not, then ..."

"It would be interesting, and perhaps instructive, to observe his reaction when he was told?" Holmes finished.

"Just so, Mr Holmes. Now, shall we have him up here?" and the Superintendent called out an order to one of his subordinates. As we waited for Gerard to brought up, Superintendent Ingham added, "I'll let you start the ...

questions, Mr Holmes, if you like? But I must reserve the right to ask what I like at any time."

"That is very kind," said Holmes, "and very fair."

A moment later, and a constable brought Mr Charles Gerard into the room. He was a tall young man, no more than twenty-three or twenty-four years of age, good looking enough in a weak sort of way. He looked as if he had not slept much the previous night, and his face bore signs of genuine grief, or I was very much mistaken. As Superintendent Ingham told him, civilly enough, to take a seat, I reflected sadly that the late Mrs Gerard could hardly have been much older than her husband, and I sighed to myself at the tragic waste of life, irrespective of who might, or might not, have killed her.

Superintendent Ingham was saying to Gerard, "This is Mr Sherlock Holmes, who happens to be in Singapore, and who is interested in this matter."

"Sherlock Holmes?" It was evident that Gerard was familiar with the name of the famous detective. "Why, I've read all the accounts of your cases, sir. I don't suppose ... no, you cannot be Doctor Watson, sir?" This last addressed to me.

"I am, sir, at your service."

Gerard put a hand to his brow. "But ... but this is amazing. Tell me, Mr Holmes, who has secured your services? My brother-in-law, perhaps?"

"Insofar as I have a client," said Holmes, "it is Mr Tigran Sarkies, a friend of Mr and Mrs Masterton's."

"Oh, the manager at the Raffles Hotel? Yes, I see." Gerard put his head in his hands, and sat like that for a moment, then he straightened up, and looked at Holmes. "I am sorry, Mr Holmes, but I have been much troubled. I am glad you are here, sir, for now we might be able to find the true murderer of my wife, Emily." He nodded towards Ingham. "The Superintendent here seems to think that I did it, and I have not yet had the opportunity to put the alternative view to him."

"Well, you have the chance now," said Holmes. "Do you object if I put a few questions to you? I must tell you that you can refuse, for I have no official standing here, but Superintendent Ingham has kindly indicated that I may assist him in his attempts to get to the bottom of your wife's murder."

Gerard nodded. "Ask whatever you like, sir, and I shall answer. Anything to find the murderer of my dear wife."

"I am pleased to hear you say as much," said Holmes with a nod. "Let us begin with your marriage. When exactly did that take place?"

"Late September last year," said Gerard with a groan. "Scarcely four months ago, sir. And now ..."

"Yes, yes. And the wedding took place in London?"

Gerard nodded miserably. "St Mark's, Piccadilly."

"Ah. "Small but fashionable", I think is the phrase used by gossip column writers?"

"It was only a small wedding," Gerard agreed. "A few friends, my wife's and mine. Neither of us had any family in England, my late wife's only living relatives being her sister, Anya, now Mrs Masterton, and Derek Masterton. As to its being fashionable ... well, my wife, my late wife, that is, was quite wealthy in her own right."

"Oh?"

"And I am not." It was a statement of fact, and almost defiant. "I might just as well say it before you do."

Holmes held up a hand. "Nobody is making accusations, sir. Tell me, did Mr and Mrs Masterton attend the wedding?"

"No." Gerard seemed to hesitate. "I first met Miss Emily Cardell, as she then was, in the June of last year. We hit it off at once, and determined to marry soon afterwards. Had her sister and brother-in-law lived in England, of course, they would have been invited, but as it was, we decided that the simplest thing to do was to marry, and send them a letter saying that it was done."

"I see. So you did not tell them in advance of the ceremony?"

"As I said, we decided at fairly short notice, and were married by special licence."

Holmes asked, "And had you yourself ever met either Mr or Mrs Masterton before you arrived here?"

Gerard shook his head. "I knew about them only from what Emily told me. They had been married in England, I understand, but that was a year ago, or a little more. Before ever I met Emily."

"H'mm. So, you were married, and then you decided to come here to Singapore, to seek your fortune?"

Gerard flushed. "Not immediately, no. I had no regular employment ... I had tried my hand at one or two things without much success ... and when we married I decided to buckle down in earnest and support Emily in the proper manner. I was not desirous of living on her money, you understand? But ... well, frankly, things still worked out no better. As I say, Emily had her own money, inherited from her father, and she wanted to use the capital to start up some sort of business. But ... well, I'm an independent sort of person, and I wasn't having any of that. Finally, we compromised. I allowed Emily to use some of her money to pay our fare out here, and she would then ask her sister to put in a word for me and ask her husband to give me a job."

Holmes held up a hand. "You say you *allowed* your wife to pay your fares here?"

Gerard nodded assent.

"Tell me, whose was the original suggestion that you should come here?"

Gerard frowned. "How d'you mean, Mr Holmes?"

"Well, did you suggest that you come here and ask for a job, or was it your wife who made the suggestion? Can you not remember?"

Gerard frowned, as if struggling to recall the details. "Yes, now you mention it, it was Emily who first broached the matter. As I recall, she said something like, 'Why didn't I try a new country, a new career, a whole new direction?' I had no good reason why not, and let her persuade me. And let her pay the fares, although I had said at the outset that I didn't want any of her money." He shrugged his shoulders. "And that's what happened. We came here with the intention that Emily would talk to Derek Masterton and persuade him to give me a job."

"And did she do so?"

Gerard shrugged. "I believe she mentioned the matter to Anya Masterton, who in turn had a word with Derek. Truth to tell, I don't know how keen he was on the notion, for he didn't exactly welcome me with open arms when first we met. I took it that he was upset, felt slighted, because we had married without asking his advice or permission, though he's not a blood relative. But I'm sure he would have come round."

Superintendent Ingham, who had been smoking in silence thus far, stirred. "You say your wife was wealthy?"

"I did."

"And who gets her money now?"

Gerard gave a taut smile. "I wondered who would ask that one. I told you, I have an independent turn of mind. Oh, I didn't mind her asking Derek Masterton to give me a job, and if he had given me one, I'd have done it to the best of my ability. But I didn't want to be beholden to him, or to anyone else. So I asked Emily to make out a will as soon as we were man and wife. Her money ... and there's a lot of it ... goes to her sister, Anya Masterton."

"Does it, indeed? " asked the Superintendent thoughtfully.

"So you see," said Charles Gerard, with more spirit than he had thus far shown, "I had no motive for killing my wife. Her money, that I might have used ... if I had wanted to ... if Emily had lived, goes elsewhere; her brother-in-law has no reason to give me a job ... unless he is overcome by an unexpected excess of sentimentality. And for good measure, I am alone, friendless, penniless, in a strange land, and have just lost my wife. Anything else? Oh, I forgot ... I am under arrest for murder!"

"Now, now," said Ingham sternly, "no need to take that tone, sir. I'm only doing my job, you know. And you must confess that it looks bad for you. Unless, that is, you might be able to suggest someone else who would want to kill your wife?"

Gerard looked hopelessly at the Superintendent, and for a moment I thought that he was about to break down. Then he pulled himself together with an obvious effort, and shook his head slowly. "No, I admit that I cannot," he said. "And I'm sorry about my little outburst just now, but things have been a touch trying. No, that's the damnable thing about it. Nobody that I can think of had any reason to kill Emily."

Superintendent Ingham cleared his throat with every appearance of embarrassment. "You say that your wife's sister will inherit ..."

"No!" It was forceful to the point of vehemence. "Why, apart from the fact that the very idea is revolting, Anya Masterton is a wealthy woman in her own right, for the late Mr Cardell, their father, left the two girls well provided for financially. And then Derek Masterton is himself a respected and successful businessman, as you should know, Superintendent."

Holmes interjected, "How did your late wife get on with her sister?"

"With Anya? Very well. They were hugging and kissing when we first got here, evidently delighted to see one another after a fairly long absence. Emily had never been here to Singapore, you see, so they had not seen one another since Anya married Derek in England." He frowned at Holmes. "You surely cannot suspect Anya? As I say, and will keep on saying, the very notion is not merely repulsive but ridiculous."

Ingham nodded slowly. "All that you say is quite true, sir. But you see that the truth of it only makes things look worse for you?"

Gerard put a hand to his brow. "I know that only too well," he said ruefully, "but I cannot tell you what I do not know. I only know that I can think of nobody with a reason, a motive, to kill Emily."

"Your landlady did, I think, mention that you had words with your late wife?" Holmes added innocently.

Gerard stared blankly at him. "Oh? Oh! That was merely a little difference of opinion, Mr Holmes."

"The evidence of the landlady seemed to suggest that it was a touch heated, though?"

Gerard seemed about to speak, to defend himself perhaps, but then he shrugged his shoulders, and remarked, "I can say only that it was not relevant here, sir."

"But you will not tell me the cause of the argument?"

"I will not."

"And you cannot think of anyone ... anyone at all ... with the slightest reason to wish harm to your wife?"

Gerard shook his head, with more conviction now. "I cannot, Mr Holmes. And nobody with the opportunity, that I can see." He looked earnestly at Ingham. "But, touching that point, you did not tell me just how she died, apart from suggesting some nonsense about poison?" And he stared at Ingham, with an odd look on his face.

Ingham looked in turn at Holmes and nodded his head to indicate that my old friend should take over.

Holmes said smoothly, "It does seem very much as if the late Mrs Gerard was poisoned."

"But that's rank nonsense!" Gerard cried. "We had exactly the same to eat and drink, and I haven't been poisoned." He turned and stared at me. "Doctor Watson, you're a respected medical man ... can you be certain that it was not some sort of seizure, a sudden heart attack, something of that kind?"

"I almost wish I could, sir," I told him. "There seems no doubt as to the matter."

"But ... what sort of poison? And how on earth was it administered?"

"Arsenic," said Holmes, steel in his voice.

"Good Lord!" Gerard looked as if he were about to faint. "But ... but how? Where?"

"You gave your wife a box of sugarplums, I think?" said Holmes.

"No. Oh ... those chocolate things? Yes ... but you don't mean ..."

"Arsenic was found in some of those," Holmes went on inexorably. "And arsenic was found in your wife's stomach, along with traces of some of the sugarplums. There seems little doubt as to the mechanics of the poisoning."

Gerard buried his head in his hands, and there was a long silence. Then he lifted his head with an effort, and gazed at Holmes. "You really mean that ... that somebody put arsenic in these sweetmeats?"

"In some of them, yes."

Gerard shook his head in disbelief. "I cannot believe it." And then his face changed, he looked odd, as if the terrible fact of his wife's death had been replaced by some nagging little doubt, some curious but trifling puzzle. "But you said ... *some* of the sweets, Mr Holmes?"

"Yes, and that is a singular thing. Arsenic was found in only four of the remaining sweets, all 'Violet Cremes'."

A very peculiar look came over Gerard's face. "That is more singular than you think, Mr Holmes!"

"And why, pray?"

"Because Emily hated 'Violet Cremes'."

"What's that?"

"I happen to know that Emily hated 'Violet Cremes', or anything like them. I chanced to buy her a box of chocolate 'Violet Cremes' in England, soon after we met, wanting to buy her a little present, but not knowing her well enough to buy jewellery or anything of that kind. Anyway, she took the box, but then she acted very strangely. She thanked me for the gift, but then she seemed most embarrassed. When I ventured to ask why, she tried to laugh the matter off. It was only when I had known her for a week or two and we were getting on famously that she told me that she hated the things."

Superintendent Ingham gave a sort of grunt at this point, and I knew what he was thinking. He said, "Well, sir, that's all very interesting, but it's hardly the sort of hard evidence that would sway a judge and jury, is it?"

Gerard stared at him. "Oh, I see ... you mean that I could easily have made that up?"

"You could, sir, and that's a fact. Tell me, you say that your wife disliked 'Violet Cremes', but what about 'Walnut Whirls', then? Did she like those?"

"She did, as a matter of fact," said Gerard easily enough. "Indeed, she ... oh!"

"Yes, sir?"

Gerard shook his head. He said slowly, "Emily loved walnuts, and any and all of the sweets and chocolates associated with them. As a matter of fact, I think that she ate some of the walnut sweets ... though I couldn't say just how many ... from the box that I took for her. She was opening the box as I left the room, and ate at least one of the things ... and, knowing her tastes, it would be a walnut."

"Ah!" Ingham inclined his head, and looked at Holmes and me.

"Is that significant?" asked Gerard, with every appearance of being puzzled.

Ingham ignored the question. "Still," he said, "the business about 'Violet Cremes' doesn't mean a lot, does it, sir? There's nothing more ... ah, concrete, as it were, that you can tell me, at all?"

Gerard hesitated. "There is, as a matter of fact."

"Well, sir?"

"Well ... no, it's ridiculous."

"What is?"

Gerard shook his head. "It's ridiculous, I say, but ... well, then, if you must know ... it's true that I took those sweet things to Emily. But I hadn't bought them, for I had no notion that such things existed. They were given to me to give to Emily ..." and he broke off.

"And by whom, sir?" Ingham insisted.

Gerard hesitated a moment, but it was clear that the Superintendent would not be put off this time. "Well, then," said Gerard at last, "if you really must know ... by her sister, Anya Masterton."

Chapter Five

The Redoubtable Miss Earnshaw

"What d'you think to the sister, then?" asked Superintendent Ingham, rummaging in his pockets until he found a penknife, with which to clean out his old briar pipe.

Charles Gerard had said nothing more of interest following the astonishing revelation that the poisoned sweets had been a gift from the poor victim's own sister. Nothing, that is, beyond loud and repeated protestations that Mrs Masterton could not, and would not, *et cetera*. He had now been returned to the cells, and the three of us had been sitting in silence in the Superintendent's office for some five minutes.

Holmes shook his head. "She would, of course, know that her sister had a weakness for walnuts. But equally she would know that her sister had an aversion to 'Violet Cremes'." He added thoughtfully, "That could, of course, be a bluff."

Ingham nodded. "Poison in the ones you know will be eaten, but also poison in the ones you know won't. Throw dust in the eyes of the poor old policeman by making it appear a stranger did it, that it wasn't someone who knew her tastes."

"And the same applies to Mr Gerard, of course," said Holmes.

"Of course." The Superintendent frowned. He leaned forward, and waved the stem of his pipe at us to emphasize his words. "And if the husband had inherited the lady's cash, or if there had been another woman anywhere in the case, I'd have put my money on him. As it is, I'm wondering if I arrested the wrong person altogether. The sister inherits, and that must be a strong point."

"But the sister is herself a rich woman," I pointed out.

"So it seems. But things are not always what they seem," said Ingham.

"And I never yet met a rich man ... or woman ... who refused a little more," added Holmes with a laugh. "Superintendent, I observe that you have that modern amenity, the telephone. I wonder if it is worth contacting Mr Tigran Sarkies at the Raffles Hotel and asking if he knows whether Mrs Masterton is yet in any condition to answer a few questions?"

Ingham nodded, and lifted the receiver. He spoke for a moment or two, then replaced the telephone, and raised an eyebrow. "Mr Sarkies tells me that the doctor has just been to see Mrs Masterton, and given her another sedative. She won't be able to talk to us until tomorrow, by what I gather."

"H'mm. That is rather inconvenient," said Holmes.

"For us," Ingham told his pipe in an aside, smiling significantly.

Holmes laughed. "Meaning that it is not necessarily so for Mrs Derek Masterton? Yes, I take your point. What of Mr Masterton? Is it worth considering him?"

Ingham frowned. "The wife inherits the money, so the husband has a motive, you mean? I haven't heard that he's short of money, or in any sort of business difficulty, though. Remember we're a fairly small, close-knit community out here, and it's hard to keep things like that secret. However, we can at least talk to him, and perhaps make some discreet enquiries at the bank and so forth."

Holmes nodded. "But first I might take a look at the room where Mrs Gerard died?"

"If you wish," said Ingham. "But there was, I assure you, nothing there of any consequence."

Holmes sighed theatrically.

"And besides," Ingham added, "the landlady will have cleaned the rooms by now, I expect."

Holmes cast his eyes to the heavens. "Ah, would that the scene of the crime might ... just once ... be left untouched," he said.

Ingham shrugged his shoulders. "Well, it can't be helped. We do have Mrs Gerard's effects here, if they'd be of any interest?"

"Any papers, personal documents?"

"Ah!" Ingham flushed slightly. "Again, there has been so little time, and especially when the culprit seemed so glaringly obvious."

"A handbag, perhaps?" suggested Holmes, turning his head to look at me, and raising an eyebrow ever so slightly.

Ingham nodded, and called out an instruction to one of his subordinates. The man returned in a moment, bringing with him a large red leather handbag, which he passed over the desk to Ingham. The Superintendent opened it, and rummaged inside. "The usual things. Ah, here's a diary." He passed it to Holmes. "Oh, and some sort of note, or letter. Addressed to Mrs Gerard in block capitals, but no postage stamps or anything, so it was evidently delivered by hand."

He opened the envelope, took out a single sheet of paper, and read aloud, "'Mrs Gerard ... Please be so kind as to meet me in the Long Bar at the Raffles Hotel on Friday, at 5-30 pm. I shall be in the corner opposite the door, but you can always ask the waiters, they'll know me. Please also have the great kindness to bring the amount we agreed, namely £50 (sterling.) Yours very sincerely, HE'. Fifty pounds, eh?"

Holmes nodded. I may perhaps remind you that fifty pounds in 1905 was not by any means what fifty pounds is in these days, but was a substantial amount, representing a few months' pay for a working man. "Blackmail, d'you think?" he suggested. "A discarded lover, something of that kind?"

"Sounds remarkably like it to me," said Ingham. He frowned. "Though I'd thought that Mrs Gerard didn't know anyone in Singapore?"

"Perhaps this 'HE' came over on the same boat?" I said tentatively. "Someone she'd known back in London?"

"A distinct possibility," said Holmes with a nod. "Tell me," he asked Ingham, "does 'HE' not suggest anyone to you?"

Ingham thought. "There's one or two, sir. Herbert Everard, for one. But he's a judge. Can't see him being a blackmailer."

"Some ambassador?" I suggested. "The 'HE' might be an honorific, not his initials?"

Ingham shook his head. "I can't see that, Doctor. I hardly like to think badly of a diplomat." He smiled, then, "Oh! Harry Ellis?"

"And who might he be?" asked Holmes.

"Same line as you and me, so to speak," said Ingham. "He's a private enquiry agent." It was said easily enough, but there was an odd note in his voice as he spoke, and Holmes and I regarded him closely.

Ingham shrugged his shoulders. "He's not exactly out of the top drawer," he said. "I've had my eye on him more than once, I can tell you. Nothing proved against him, mark you, I don't say there has been. But ... well, once or twice I've had my doubts about him."

"Blackmail?" suggested Holmes.

Ingham nodded slowly. "That, and one or two other small matters. Nothing to attract my attention officially, you understand, just ... irregularities, shall we say? Harry has what they call an eye to the main chance, I'm afraid."

"Ah!" Holmes glanced at his watch. "I see that it is almost four o'clock. I suggest that we go downstairs and ask Mr Gerard if he knows anything about this note, or anything of Mr Harry Ellis. And then I think we might adjourn to the Long Bar, first for a drink, and second to see who might turn up."

"But won't this 'HE', whoever it might be, know of Mrs Gerard's death, and fail to turn up?" I asked.

Holmes looked at Ingham. The Superintendent shook his head. "No danger there, for I've kept it quiet for the moment, Doctor. No report has appeared in the papers, so unless this 'HE' has been to the lodging house, then he ... or she ... won't know of Mrs Gerard's death."

"Unless, that is ..." said Holmes, and left it at that.

"H'mm. In which case his absence would be significant? Well, we'll see." Ingham stood up, and led us downstairs to the cells.

It was stifling down there – no open windows or electric fans for these poor devils, and noisy, too, for there were groans, yells and curses in every language that I knew, and a few that I didn't.

Gerard had been given the luxury of his own cell, dark and oven-like though it was. He was sitting on his bunk, his head in his hands. He looked up with dull eyes as Holmes entered the little cell. "Well, Mr Holmes?"

Holmes held out the letter in its envelope. "Do you recognize this, sir?"

Gerard shook his head. "No. Should I?" He glanced a second time at the envelope and frowned. "Addressed to Emily? No, I ..." and he broke off.

"You do not recollect its being delivered to your late wife since you arrived in Singapore?"

Gerard shook his head. "But then, I haven't been ... I mean, I wasn't with her all the time at the lodging house. I went to see Derek Masterton once or twice, and left Emily there. It might perhaps have been delivered to her during one of my absences?"

"Very likely," said Holmes. "Tell me, do the initials 'HE' suggest anything to you?"

"His Excellency? Isn't that what they style ambassadors, or governors or something?"

"And the name Ellis, then? Harry Ellis? D'you know anyone of that name?"

"Not at all," said Gerard, a bewildered look on his face.

Holmes nodded. "Thank you." He made as if to leave the cell and then turned back. "You still decline to tell me anything about the quarrel you had with your wife?"

"I do. Beyond reiterating that it had nothing to do with the present matter."

"Very well. And you said that the sweets were given to you by Mrs Anya Masterton?"

Gerard nodded. "But as I told you, the notion that Anya might have killed Emily is quite ridiculous."

"Perhaps so. Never the less, humour me. Tell me, if you would, the precise circumstances under which the sweets were given to you."

Gerard frowned. "I went to see Derek Masterton yesterday morning, at his home. We ..."

"Your late wife remained behind?" Holmes interjected.

Gerard frowned. "She did. As you said yourself, we'd had ... that is to say, things were a bit uneasy between us just then. We'd arranged to visit Derek and Anya, and I reminded Emily of the fact; but she pleaded a headache. I may say I wasn't entirely convinced, but ..." and he shrugged his shoulders. "If you gentlemen are married, or have been, you'll understand."

"Of course," said Holmes – a lifelong bachelor! "But you were saying?"

"Oh, yes. I went to the Mastertons, and we had a chat. I was tempted to broach the matter of my entering Derek's firm, but didn't ..."

"And why not?" Holmes added quickly.

Gerard shrugged. "It didn't seem appropriate. I told you, I was waiting for Emily to put a word in for me. Anyway, we talked about Singapore, and about Masterton's business ... in a general sort of way only ... and everything seemed fine. Then he excused himself, said he had another appointment and asked if I wanted a lift anywhere. I said no, I was just passing time, so he left. I was about to say farewell to Mrs Masterton, when she asked if everything was all right between me and Emily. I don't know how she knew, perhaps Emily had said something when last the two of them met; or perhaps Mrs Masterton just sensed something in my behaviour which said all was not well. Anyway, I tried to laugh it off, but in the end I admitted we'd had a bit of a tiff.

Anya told me not to be silly, to go and make things right with Emily and buy her a present on the way back. I must have looked blank, because Anya said something like, 'Oh, wait a moment', and went out of the room. She came back a moment later with that damned box of sugarplums and told me to give them to Emily saying that they were from me."

"And you did."

Gerard nodded. "I did just that." He shook his head, as if he could not believe what was happening to him. "But ..." and he looked intently at me. "Doctor Watson, are you absolutely sure ..."

"I'm afraid so," I told him.

"But it's incredible? Unbelievable." He shook his head again. "No," he said, decidedly, "I cannot believe it. I will not believe it. There has been some ghastly mistake, gentlemen, mark my words."

"But you cannot suggest the nature of this *mistake* at all?" asked Holmes gently.

Gerard stared at him for a moment and then shook his head without speaking.

"You gave your wife the box of sugarplums on your return from the Mastertons?"

Gerard nodded. "That was around half past eleven, possibly twelve noon."

"You said, I recall, that she ate one immediately?"

"Yes ... no! She thanked me, and opened the box, but did not eat any just then. Or did she?" He put a hand to his brow. "I think she took one out, but then replaced it. I honestly cannot be sure."

"The point is interesting, but not essential. Pray continue," said Holmes.

"Well, Emily seemed in a better mood, and I asked if her headache had gone, and she said it was better, but still slightly troublesome. She said she did not want any luncheon, or to go out. I didn't particularly want to stay inside, but I thought I ought to stay there with Emily. She, however, insisted that I go out and enjoy myself. Enjoy myself! I ..." and he broke off, and rubbed a hand over his eyes.

"I understand that it is very hard for you," Holmes told him softly. "But I must ask these things. You went out and had some lunch, perhaps?"

Gerard nodded. "And then I went back to see how Emily was. That would be around five in the afternoon." He stopped, and let out something very like a sob of anguish.

"And ... forgive me, but I must ask this ... who found your wife's body?" asked Holmes gently.

Gerard winced at the question, and did not speak for a while. Then, "I did," he said with an obvious effort.

"And you were, of course, greatly distressed. But tell me, what exactly did you do?"

"Do? I went for the police, of course." Gerard stared at Holmes, an angry look in his eye. Then he subsided. "No, I ran out of the room, and downstairs. I shouted something or other to the landlady, who was hanging about in the hallway, and then ... I was distraught, you know ... then I ran out into the street, with some half-baked notion of finding a policeman out there, I suppose. There was no policeman in sight, only the usual throng of folk wandering past all unknowing and uncaring that Emily ... well! And so then I went back inside, calmed down a little, and asked the landlady to telephone for the police."

Ingham nodded. "We got the news from the landlady, as Mr Gerard says, and went round at once."

"H'mm. And the landlady and maids and so on had not seen any strangers, any visitors or anyone acting suspiciously? Anyone who should not have been there?"

Ingham shook his head. "But then the place ... well, forgive me, Mr Gerard, but it isn't exactly the Raffles Hotel, you know! Anyone could have lurked by the front door until the hallway was empty, and sneaked in. And similarly they could wait on the upstairs landing until the coast was clear to get back out again. And then even if they had been seen, the servants and so on would just have thought they were visiting, or perhaps even that they were lodging there. As I say, it's that sort of place. A bit informal, as you might say."

"And so, in all that informality, nobody was in fact seen?"

"No, sir."

"Well, I think that is all for the moment." Holmes nodded to the superintendent, and we left the cell. My blood ran cold as the door was flung shut, and the key scraped in the lock. If Gerard really were a murderer, then he was as callous a one as ever I encountered, and a brilliant actor to boot. If he were innocent, then what must be going through his mind as he sat there in the half-darkness, bereft of his new wife and suspected of her murder? I pulled myself together with a considerable effort, and followed Superintendent Ingham up the stairs towards the charge room and the street door.

"So," said Ingham, as we went along the corridor, "Mrs Gerard pleaded a headache, did she? And sent Mr Gerard out to enjoy himself while she stayed in alone."

"Expecting the note from 'HE', and waiting in for it, you mean?" said Holmes.

"Just so."

"It certainly sounds that way. Of course, if 'HE' had gone in person, he ... or she ... would hardly need to send the note."

"That's true," said Ingham. "But if the bearer of the note got in unobserved, anyone else could. That makes things look a little better for Mr Gerard."

"But not much?"

"Well, sir, Mrs Gerard might have had that letter in her bag for a couple of days," said Ingham. "It said 'meet me on Friday', as I recall, and not 'tomorrow', didn't it? The letter might even have been delivered in London, before ever she left."

Holmes nodded. "True enough." He added with a smile, "Although the paper is most definitely not of English manufacture."

"Oh?"

"I will stake my reputation on it. But, as you say, the note might have been delivered at any time from Monday."

As we passed the desk behind which stood a couple of uniformed officers, one of the sergeants called out to Ingham, "Beg pardon, Superintendent, but this lady is asking to see you." And in a lower tone, he added, "Very insistent she is, too."

"Oh?" Ingham looked where the sergeant had nodded, and I followed his example, to see a young woman sitting on one of the hard and none too clean wooden benches. She was around twenty years of age, not what I could call beautiful in any conventional sense, but handsome enough to make any man look twice, with a face that betokened resolution and determination. Her hair was, in the hackneyed phrase of the poets, 'her crowning glory', for her long auburn tresses fell almost to her waist in great luxuriant swathes, so that, given a somewhat weaker, a more ethereal, face, she might have served as a model for one of the pre-Raphaelites.

The Superintendent had taken one look at this young woman, and said, "Oh!" in an undertone, as if he recognized her. Holmes and I followed Ingham as he strode across the room.

At his approach, the woman stood up. "Ah, Superintendent Ingham." And she held out her hand, for all the world as one man holds his hand out to another.

"Miss Earnshaw, how nice to see you again." The Superintendent took her hand, but instead of shaking it, he – much to my delight – kissed it, like some great clumsy courtier, causing Miss Earnshaw to flush slightly.

"Miss Earnshaw, may I present Mr Sherlock Holmes, and Doctor John Watson? Gentlemen, Miss Margaret Earnshaw."

"I am delighted to meet you, gentlemen," said Miss Earnshaw in an abstracted fashion. "You will, I am sure, excuse my apparent rudeness, but I should be most grateful for a moment's conversation with Superintendent Ingham here."

Holmes and I muttered something appropriate, but the Superintendent took Miss Earnshaw by the arm, moved a few paces into the corner where it was marginally quieter, and said in a low tone, "These gentlemen are friends of Mr Tigran Sarkies, and looking into … you know."

"Oh!" Miss Earnshaw regarded us with more interest, if not actual respect, on hearing this.

Ingham said, "We'd be better off in my room. More discreet there."

"Of course." Miss Earnshaw allowed the Superintendent to lead her back the way we had just come, and Holmes and I followed along meekly.

Once in the Superintendent's room, Ingham waved us to chairs. He looked at Holmes and me. "I should perhaps tell you that Miss Earnshaw here is governess to the Masterton children." And to Miss Earnshaw, he said, "I take it that this dreadful business of Mrs Gerard brings you here?"

Miss Earnshaw nodded. "It is. I heard the story, or at any rate a garbled version of it, from poor Mr Masterton, who is very upset, as you may imagine. As soon as I could decently spare the time to get away from my duties I went round to the Gerards' lodgings, but the people there could tell me only that Charles ... Mr Gerard ... had been taken away by the police. So ... so then I came round here." And she sat upright in her chair, staring at Ingham if inviting him to respond.

It was Holmes who spoke first. "You are governess to the two Masterton children?" he asked.

"As Mr Ingham here has just said."

"Are they not rather young for a governess? As I understood it, the Mastertons have been married but two years."

"Rather less, in point of fact," replied Miss Earnshaw coolly. "The elder boy is just over a year old, the younger quite a baby, three months only." She smiled and Holmes looked puzzled. "You see, Mr ... Holmes, was it?"

"Sherlock Holmes, madam." Holmes looked rather nettled that his name should not immediately be familiar to Miss Earnshaw.

Somewhat to my dismay – for it does Holmes no real harm to be taken down a peg occasionally – Miss Earnshaw frowned, and then her face cleared. "Oh! The famous detective ... I had thought you were ... ah, quite retired, sir."

"The reports of my retirement, like those of Mark Twain's death, are much exaggerated," said Holmes, still not entirely happy with this absence of the acclamation he felt due to him.

"Be that as it may," Miss Earnshaw continued blithely, "Anya ... Mrs Masterton ... had a succession of nurses, nannies and governesses as a child, and so she determined that any children of hers would have the same guiding hand throughout their childhood, if it were possible. Give the little darlings some steadiness and stability, as it were. Very sensible, too. As a matter of fact, there is a nurse as well, a local girl, which makes my job easier. When they get older, of course, both being boys ..." and she smiled sweetly at Holmes, who was, as always, completely unmoved.

"H'mm," said he. "I see. Forgive me, Superintendent, you were, I think, about to outline matters to Miss Earnshaw?"

"Thank you, Mr Holmes. Well, Miss Earnshaw ... and I know you're a sensible sort of lady, won't faint or any nonsense of that sort ... but the fact is that poor Mrs Gerard was poisoned."

"Oh!" Miss Earnshaw did not faint, but she did put her hands to her mouth as if to stifle a gasp of horror.

"Yes," said Ingham, "I know. A dreadful business, and no mistake."

"But ... but are you quite sure? Could it not have been some sudden illness, natural causes? Mrs Gerard was, after all, unused to the heat of the tropics?" Miss Earnshaw gazed earnestly at Ingham, as though she were willing it to be as she had suggested.

Ingham looked at me. "Doctor?"

"No doubt about it, I'm afraid," I said, as kindly as I could. "The evidence is quite conclusive as to the cause of death."

"And Charles ... Mr Gerard?"

"Well, Miss Earnshaw, just at the moment he's ... ah, helping us with our enquiries."

"You cannot mean that you have arrested him?"

Ingham looked almost embarrassed. "The fact is, Miss Earnshaw, things do look rather bad against him."

Miss Earnshaw's face coloured, giving her whole being a sort of glow of righteous indignation. "But it's arrant nonsense," she cried. "He could never have hurt a fly, much less poisoned his wife!"

"So I'm told," said Ingham imperturbably. "Never the less, it's my duty to look into it, Miss Earnshaw, and I'd be neglecting that duty if I didn't look pretty closely at Mr Gerard."

Miss Earnshaw shook her head. "I see what you are getting at, Superintendent, but I am certain that you are making a grave mistake. Tell me, how exactly do you think Mrs Gerard was poisoned?"

"It seems clear that she was given arsenic, contained in a box of sugarplums."

For a moment Miss Earnshaw simply sat there, staring at the Superintendent as if she were trying to make sense out of his words. And then, to the complete astonishment of us all, she slumped down in a dead faint.

"Quick, Watson!"

"Really, Holmes," I said, as I attended to Miss Earnshaw, "I had grasped the need for urgency as soon as I saw the lady keel over."

"Force of habit, my boy," he said with a taut smile, patting me on the back.

I soon had Miss Earnshaw back on her feet. She seemed more embarrassed at the show of weakness than actually ill, but in any event it was clear that she was in no fit state to talk to us further. Superintendent Ingham accordingly had one of his men call a cab, and we all stood in the street, rather dolefully, as that cab negotiated the crowds of vehicles and pedestrians, and took her back to the Masterton house.

Holmes turned to Ingham. "What do you know of Miss Earnshaw?" he asked him.

Ingham shrugged. "A likeable girl," he said in a paternal fashion. "She arrived here some three months ago, perhaps four, and took up the post as governess to the Mastertons' boys."

"Three months or so only?" said Holmes.

"About that." Ingham permitted himself a smile. "She would hardly have been here much longer, Mr Holmes, when the elder lad is but a year old."

"Of course. Silly of me." Holmes thought for a moment, then asked, "May I just have another very quick word with Mr Charles Gerard, do you think, Superintendent?"

"As many as you like, Mr Holmes, if you think it will do any good." And the Superintendent led us back inside the police station, and down to the cells.

I was not best pleased to have to leave the relative cool of the doorway for those baking hot cells again, and wondered vaguely what Holmes might have thought of now.

Charles Gerard was slumped on his bunk bed when we entered his cell. He looked up and frowned. "Back again, Mr Holmes?"

"Just a couple of questions, if you will. Tell me," asked Holmes, "are you acquainted with a Miss Margaret Earnshaw?"

"Maggie? Of course. She's the Mastertons' governess, or their childrens', rather."

"Ah, but I had the distinct impression that you had known her for a longer time than the four days that you have been in Singapore?"

"Oh, yes," said Gerard readily. "I've known Maggie ... what? Ten years? About that."

"You knew her back in England, then?"

Gerard nodded. "As a matter of fact, it was Maggie who first introduced me to Emily. The two of them had been friends for years, although I myself had never met Emily before last summer."

"H'mm. And were you and Miss Earnshaw ... ah, good friends?"

Holmes said the words easily enough and innocently enough, but Charles Gerard did not answer immediately. Instead, he flushed slightly, and gazed down at his shoes, from which the laces had been officially removed.

"Mr Gerard?"

"As a matter of fact, I was quite keen on her at one time, and I think she was keen on me."

"But you did not press the matter?"

Gerard tried to laugh. "The old difficulty, I'm afraid. Neither of us had any money to speak of, and I didn't want a wife of mine to live in poverty. So we sort of drifted away from one another. That would be, oh, a couple of years ago? And then, last year, I ran into Maggie again, quite unexpectedly, and she said that she had a friend, someone she wanted me to meet, and would I buy them luncheon one day. I did, and the friend turned out to be Emily. We hit it off at once, and that was that."

"I see. And how came Miss Earnshaw to leave England three months ago to work for your sister-in-law?"

"Oh that was Emily's doing. She happened to mention to Maggie that Anya Masterton was looking out for a respectable governess for her boys, and Maggie said she wouldn't mind applying for the post. Next thing I knew, Maggie was taking the boat to Singapore." He gazed at Holmes. "But why are you asking these questions, Mr Holmes? I have the uneasy feeling that there is some ulterior motive, and that someone has come under suspicion. I trust that you don't think that Maggie and I ..."

"No, no." Holmes waved a hand. "It is my job ... and perhaps, too, a part of my nature ... to wonder, to theorize, to speculate, to ask questions. Sometimes my job is far from agreeable, and no more are the questions." He turned to go. "Well, sir, I shall not bother you further. Pray do not lose hope, for my investigations are still in their early stages, and much may yet come to light."

Ingham and I followed Holmes as he led the way out into the street. Holmes paused in the doorway, and at first I thought he had been taken aback by the heat or the crowds. But he merely glanced rather indolently at his watch. "H'mm, we have been somewhat distracted from our original plan," said he. "We shall not have time for a leisurely drink at the Long Bar after all, and indeed if we are not to miss our appointment entirely, we must hasten there at once."

Chapter Six

We Keep an Appointment

As we made our way through the crowded and noisy streets, Superintendent Ingham remarked, "Well, gentlemen, and what d'you think of all that? I did say, if you remember, that if there were another woman in the case, things would look even worse for Mr Gerard. And now here she is, in the shape of Miss Maggie Earnshaw." He sighed. "Not the first time it's happened, either. Two young people, too poor to marry, lay their plans. One of 'em marries for money, then they conspire to bump off the poor wife ... or poor husband, as the case may be ... and take up where they left off. If ever they did leave off."

"My dear Superintendent," I said loftily, as I circled round a cart piled high with exotic fruits and vegetables, "Miss Earnshaw was as surprised to learn that those sugarplums contained arsenic as I was. Why, she fainted clear away when you told her."

Ingham shrugged. "Maybe she's just a very good actress?" he suggested.

I shook my head. "Her faint was real enough, or I never attended a lecture at medical school."

"Well, then, perhaps she was just shocked to learn that the poison, or its means of administration, had been found so readily? Remember, Miss Earnshaw is governess at the Mastertons', lives in the house, so she could have doctored the sugarplums easily enough."

Even I could see the logical flaw in that one. "But by no stretch of the imagination could she have induced Mrs Masterton to give the box of sugarplums to Charles Gerard to pass on to his wife," I cried, waving aside a fellow who was trying to sell me a brace of live hens.

"More to the point," Holmes interjected, "there is the matter of Mrs Gerard's will, wherein she left her fortune to her sister, and not to her husband. If these two young people were in it only for the money, as it were, they have handled the matter very strangely, have they not?"

"H'mm, that's true enough," said Ingham.

Holmes frowned, and made as if to speak, but anything he might have tried to say was lost in the din, as a hundred different speakers roared at one another in a dozen different languages.

"What's that?" I yelled at Holmes, at a temporary lull in the uproar.

"We must do two things as soon as may be," said Holmes. "One, find out if Miss Earnshaw was in the Masterton house yesterday when Mr Gerard called, for it may indeed be that she might somehow have induced Mrs Masterton to give him the poisoned sweetmeats … a casual suggestion, that is not so very hard to believe, surely? If Mrs Masterton trusted her, relied upon her advice … h'mm. Two, we must find out if Miss Earnshaw knew the contents of Mrs Gerard's will."

"But," said Ingham, "if the two of them were in it together, Charles Gerard might have told Miss Earnshaw, in which case they would deny the fact. Oh," he added gloomily, "that won't do, for if they were in it, as you say, sir, then why should Mr Gerard ask his wife to leave her money to her sister?"

"We have only his word that he did so," said Holmes. "It may, for all we know be to the contrary and have been Mrs Gerard's own idea ... if, for example, she had suspicions of her husband's fidelity, or his intentions."

"Heavens, that's true, Mr Holmes!"

"Then was the will actually signed? Is it valid? For if not, then Mr Gerard would inherit. Unless, that is, he hangs for murder," added Holmes with a grim smile. "And then it may have been that Charles Gerard is indeed innocent of any wrong doing, but that Miss Earnshaw is not, that she was acting independently. She is a strong personality, when all is said and done. But here we are at the Raffles Hotel. Let us see who is waiting for us, before we start to speculate."

As we made our way through to the Long Bar, I was struck once again by the lightness and comfort of the place, by the contrast with the noisy and bustling streets outside, and perhaps more particularly by the very marked contrast to the dark cell in which the unfortunate Charles Gerard was now residing.

I shook myself, if only metaphorically. It was only the afternoon, but I had the sensation of having endured a long day, and a confusing one – but then please remember, if you will, that Holmes and I had only set foot on dry land earlier that day following our lengthy sea voyage. Then the hustle and bustle of the packed streets, to say nothing of our investigation. We had indeed been plunged headlong into a strange and sinister business. Yes, it had been a long and busy day for us. And I, for one, was ready for a drink, and a little quiet meditation. Not, I reflected, that I was likely to get much time for peaceful and gentle meditation where Holmes was concerned. I looked at my old friend as I thought this, and was amused to see the expression on his face, for all the world like an old hunting dog that scents the quarry and is eager for the chase.

The Long Bar was dark, cool, and surprisingly busy for the time of day, as it seemed to me. Planters, merchants, the whole of Singapore's busy community seemed to have dropped in for a quick drink. Superintendent Ingham paused just inside the door, and glanced over at the far side of the room. "Ahah!" he muttered.

"Mr Ellis?" asked Holmes.

"Yes, just as I suspected."

I followed Ingham's gaze, and saw a short, stout man seated on his own at a small table in a far corner. His white suit was none too clean, his narrow tie was positively sordid, and his Panama hat had seen better days. The Superintendent was right, I thought, Mr Harry Ellis could not, by any stretch of the imagination, be described as out of the top drawer.

Ingham led the way over to the little table. At his approach, Ellis glanced up, and at the sight of the policeman his face fell, or I was much mistaken. But he recovered quickly, smiled broadly, and greeted Ingham cheerily. "Superintendent, how pleasant to see you."

"Is it, indeed?"

"Oh, indeed it is." Ellis looked quickly at Holmes and me, and gave a quick little smile. "Gentlemen, nice to see you."

"Harry, I haven't introduced you," said Ingham, a slow smile developing on his face. "Gentlemen, meet Mr Harry Ellis, a well-known character in these parts. Harry, this is Mr

Sherlock Holmes, the famous London detective, and this other gentleman is Doctor John Watson, the writer."

For a moment Ellis stared at Holmes, and then he half-rose, and bobbed a little bow. "Mr Holmes, this is an honour, and Doctor Watson, too." He glanced at Ingham. "You know, for a moment I thought the Superintendent here was pulling my leg, playing a little joke on poor Harry Ellis."

"No joke, Mr Ellis," said Holmes suavely. "On the contrary, Doctor Watson and I are here on a very serious matter."

"Oh? Well, Mr Holmes, I'm sure you have your own methods, and will get along very well without my help," said Ellis, a puzzled frown on his brow. "And, if I may be so bold as to speak plainly, I have a little matter of my own in hand just at present." He took out a battered silver watch, and glanced at it. "In fact, if you would have the very great kindness to excuse me, gentlemen, I'm expecting a client any moment now. Of course, Mr Holmes, should you later find that you need my assistance in any way, then ..."

"Cut it out, Harry," said the Superintendent, sitting down heavily at the little table.

"Superintendent?" Ellis still wore the puzzled look.

Holmes interjected, "You evidently mistake my meaning, Mr Ellis. The fact is, we are looking into the murder of Mrs Charles Gerard."

"What?" It came out almost as a shout, and people at neighbouring tables glanced round, shrugged, and laughed, as folk will under such circumstances. Ellis lowered his voice, and asked, "Do you really mean to tell me that Mrs Gerard has been murdered, Mr Holmes? Superintendent?"

Holmes and Ingham nodded in unison. Ingham said, "It's true, I'm afraid, Harry."

Holmes asked, "Are we correct in thinking that Mrs Gerard was the client you are ... or were, rather ... here to meet?"

Ellis nodded unhappily.

"And she was to pay you fifty pounds?" There was a good deal of scepticism in Ingham's voice.

Ellis looked hurt. "Professional fees, Superintendent!" He looked at Holmes. "I'm sure you'd have charged a good deal more, sir ... not that you wouldn't have earned it."

"Fifty pounds is a handsome fee," mused Holmes.

"I did a handsome bit of work, sir," said Ellis. He took a little leather notebook from his pocket, and waved it in the air. "All itemized, ready for Mrs Gerard's approval. And I paid out a great deal from my own pocket, money which it doesn't look as if I'll get back now," he added somewhat ungrammatically.

"Oh? Well, Mr Ellis, since your original client is regrettably not in any position to pay your fees, perhaps we should join forces to some extent? I cannot promise anything in the way of full payment, but I am certain that *my* client will not prove ungenerous, should you be able to help us in any way."

Ellis' face cleared at this. "It's kind of you to say so, Mr Holmes."

"A drink?" suggested Holmes, waving to summon a waiter.

Ellis waited until a full glass was set before him to replace the empty one already there. He lifted it to his lips, then thought better of it and set the drink down un-tasted. "Later, perhaps," he muttered to nobody in particular. Then he looked at Holmes and smiled. "Well, sir, I'll begin at the beginning, if you please, and you can just ask any questions that come to you."

"Very well."

"Well, then, the first I ever heard of Mrs Gerard was last year. I received a long letter, posted in London, from her, in which she said that she'd got my name and address from an acquaintance, a former client ... her name is neither here nor there. Anyway, I was to do a certain job of work for her, Mrs Gerard, in the discreet enquiry line. I was to invoice her for expenses, and she would not quibble at any reasonable amount either. She enclosed a banker's draft for a little something on account, which was all very good of her, and gave me all the relevant details, or at any rate such as she had, to act as my starting point. Well, Mr Holmes, I ask you, would you have tuned down a job on those terms? I hardly think so, sir, and no more did I."

Holmes nodded. "And you made the enquiries which Mrs Gerard had requested?"

"I did, sir. I sent a note agreeing to her terms, and said that I would send such information that I managed to acquire. Now, Mrs Gerard wrote back almost by return, allowing for the distance, that is, and told me that I shouldn't bother to do that, but that she herself would be in Singapore by the time that I had finished my work, and would collect the information in person. All I had to do was work away, and send her a note when I had uncovered anything."

"And you did, and Mrs Gerard came here?"

Ellis nodded. "I sent word when I was finished, or as good as, and then I got a note from her on Wednesday, to say she and her husband had just landed, and she could meet me at any time that was convenient to me. I was to let her know at such-and-such an address, but ... and this was underlined to reinforce it ... I was to be careful that she alone received the note making the appointment."

"And again, you complied?"

"Mrs Gerard was paying the piper, sir, and so as far as I was concerned she could call the tune. I sent a lad round with my note on the Thursday morning, and told him to be especially careful that nobody saw him enter or leave the hotel. The lodgings, I should say," he added with a touch of disdain in his voice.

"H'mm." Holmes stared into space for a moment. "The Gerards arrived here on Monday," he said at last. "We may perhaps give them that one day to recover their land-legs, as it were, after the lengthy sea voyage. But I wonder why Mrs Gerard did not let you know on the Tuesday that she was in Singapore, Mr Ellis?"

Ellis shrugged his shoulders. "If it was to be all on the quiet, Mr Holmes, perhaps she was busy meeting her family and all the rest of it? Couldn't get a private moment to write a little private note?"

"Well done, Mr Ellis. That is, of course, one possibility, and may very likely be the correct explanation," said Holmes. "Though I can think of yet another ..." and he broke off. Holmes is thick-skinned and very seldom actually embarrassed, but he seemed a touch discomforted.

"Mr Holmes?" asked Ellis, regarding my friend curiously.

"Well, then, to be plain, I was wondering if perhaps Mrs Gerard had second thoughts? Tell me, Mr Ellis, would you have known that the Gerards were in Singapore had Mrs Gerard not told you so?"

Ellis' face fell. "No, sir, I would not have known. Why, do you mean that Mrs Gerard may not have contacted me at all? That I may not have been paid? Not," he added with more than a touch of despondency in his tone, "not that I have any real prospects of payment anyway, beyond your promise to do what you can, Mr Holmes."

Holmes waved the financial point aside. "Yes, I half suspect that Mrs Gerard had second thoughts, that she was not certain that she wanted to know whatever it was you had found out, Mr Ellis."

Now, I flatter myself that I am the most long-suffering of men on this earth, but I had been fretting impatiently for some considerable time by now, and at this last gratuitous display of ambiguousness, I fear that I emitted a snort indicative of impatience and exasperation alike.

Holmes regarded me as he might regard a specimen under his magnifying glass. "Watson? Are you ready for your dinner, old chap? Or are you just feeling the heat?"

"Dinner be damned, and heat be damned, Holmes!" I burst out – understandably, you will agree. And I would have said more, much more.

But before I could elaborate, Mr Ellis stood up. "If you'll excuse me one moment, gentlemen?" And he wandered off to the cloakroom, leaving me seething with a sort of impotent fury.

I rounded on Holmes. "Really ..."

He waved me to silence. "All in good time, Watson. In fact, you can ask Mr Ellis yourself, when he has washed his hands." He sat in silence for a moment, then, "So, Mrs Gerard was planning to come here to Singapore to hear from Mr Ellis in person, was she? That rather suggests that the business about talking her husband into coming here to find work was a ruse, or at any rate that it was not the whole truth."

"And then she had second thoughts?" added Ingham. "Found she didn't want to know after all?" He regarded

Holmes curiously, and then transferred his gaze to me. "And you, Doctor Watson? What is it that bothers you?"

At that point, Ellis returned to the table and resumed his seat. Evidently he had heard Ingham's remark to me, for he said, "Yes, Doctor, you were about to say something, I fancy?"

I took a deep breath before starting. "Mr Ellis, we have heard the details of how you came to work for Mrs Gerard, and how she communicated with you and you with her. We have, as it were, the entire mechanism, the clockwork, laid out for our admiration. But what we lack is the mainspring. In a word, Mr Ellis, will you not at once tell us what it was that Mrs Gerard hired you to investigate? What did she want to know, sir?"

"Oh," said Ellis, "did I not say? Well, Doctor Watson, that is easy enough told, sir. Mrs Gerard wanted me to spare no expense to look into the ancestry, background, and business dealings of her brother-in-law, Mr Derek Masterton. Reading between the lines ... as you get to do in our line of work, Mr Holmes, you'll agree ... reading between the lines, then, gents, I got the distinct impression that Mrs Gerard suspected that Mr Derek Masterton was a wrong'un." And with that, perhaps feeling that he had done all that could reasonably be expected of him and so had earned a drink – or again perhaps he was simply feeling thirsty – Mr Harry Ellis leaned back in his chair, a satisfied smile on his face, and took a long pull at the glass which was before him.

Chapter Seven

A Story and a Search

"And is he?" Ingham and I asked together, like some music-hall act.

"Who? Oh, Masterton, you mean?" The infuriating Ellis drained his glass, placed it on the table, and gazed at it significantly.

"Another?" And Holmes signalled to a waiter.

"Thank you, sir, I won't say no." Ellis glanced round the room to make sure he was not being overheard, then leaned forward and lowered his voice before going on. "That's the thing," he told us in a hoarse whisper. "I couldn't find a thing wrong with Mr Derek Masterton. His business affairs, his private life, everything, all above reproach." And he leaned back and tapped the side of his nose in what I suppose was meant to be a significant fashion.

"But?" asked Holmes quickly.

"Ah, you're sharp, Mr Holmes, and no mistake," said Ellis admiringly. "Yes, sir, it does all sound too good to be true, doesn't it?" He came closer to us again and lowered his voice once more.

"The odd thing is, sir, that when I looked ... or tried to look, I should say ... into Mr Masterton's background, his history as it were, I came up against a brick wall. To all intents and purposes, Mr Masterton's life began three or four years ago when he first landed here in Singapore. For all my efforts ... and they were considerable efforts, too, though I say so myself ... I couldn't find any record, any trace, of him before he arrived here. Now, Mr Holmes, what do you say to that, sir?"

Holmes regarded Ellis keenly. "A false identity, then?"

"Just what I thought myself, sir." Ellis smiled complacently. "So, I contrived to meet Mr Masterton, just for a few moments, you know, and have a word or two with him, see if I couldn't get anything at all to work on. It seemed to me that I detected just a faint hint of an Australian accent in his voice, and so I contacted some of my friends and associates in Australia, to see if they turned anything up."

"And?"

Ellis seemed about to speak, and then he shrugged. "Well, Mr Holmes, it took time. Time, effort, and ... well, sir, not a little expense."

"Ah, I see. Well, Mr Ellis, in that case I myself will guarantee that your fees are met."

"Very good of you, sir."

"So, now that is settled, tell me what you found out."

"Nothing that would stand up in a court of law, I fear. But there was one little thing, an interesting line of thought, although it was only a hint. I'd given my Australian connections a description of Mr Masterton, of course, and, after much delay, I had a report back. Mostly to say they hadn't unearthed anything of value, but there was an interesting sort of footnote. It seems that the description of Mr

Masterton that I'd sent them tallies very closely with that of a man named Cedric Masters, who'd been a bit of a bad lad, or so it seems."

"Ah!"

Ellis frowned. "A curious business, too, Mr Holmes, all round. This Cedric Masters was an odd sort of chap. He'd never been in any trouble, not at first. But, when young Cedric was only nine or ten years old, his father invested the family's life savings in shares, a speculative mining scheme. Now, that's not so uncommon, but the man who was promoting the scheme knew it was no good ... in a word, sir, it was a swindle, and on a grand scale. Well, the Masters family lost everything, and so did a lot of other small investors. You can call them 'mugs', if you like, it's accurate enough, I suppose, but they had believed in the rogue who swindled them. Anyway, this crooked promoter apologized, said he'd acted in good faith, stressed that it was a speculation and what have you, and the investors had no means of proving otherwise, so he couldn't be touched, though the police had their suspicions. Anyway, he ... the crook, I mean ... started up another business, only this time the public didn't subscribe to it. As you might have guessed, I suppose, having had their fingers burned once. And old Masters, Cedric's father, he couldn't invest if he wanted to, for the shock, the loss, had set him back, and he didn't live for many years after things went smash. But the crook went ahead with his scheme and this time the business didn't go bust. Not a bit of it ... instead it prospered mightily."

"Ah!" said Holmes again, nodding his head. "The second business was a fake, I expect? A front to account for his wealth, wealth that was in reality the proceeds of the swindle? Yes, very clever."

Ellis nodded as well. "That's what everyone reckoned, Mr Holmes. Only there was no way of proving it, any more than there had been any way to prove the original swindle. So this crook ... and he was a crook, no doubt of that ... invested his ill-gotten gains in legitimate businesses, and prospered yet more."

"Until this Masters decided to claim that which was his? Or his family's, I should say?"

Ellis smiled. "Got it in one, Mr Holmes." He nodded. "Yes, the father died, in pretty reduced and tragic circumstances, as I say, when Cedric was fifteen or sixteen. Then some years later still, five or six years ago in fact, the crook's office was robbed, and the safe cleaned out. Fair enough, but the trouble was that the swindler was in there. Nobody knows just what happened, but he took a bullet and died at once."

Holmes whistled.

Ellis nodded again. "A bad business all round, sir. You'll likely say he got what he deserved, the crook, I mean, and I wouldn't argue with that. But then, the law's the law. Anyway, there were a couple of witnesses, Cedric was suspected, and the police got after him ... or, I should say, after the robbers, for nothing was ever proved one way or another about Masters ... but they, the police, that is, simply lost them, the fugitives. Then one of the suspects ... not this Masters, but another chap ... did turn up, and was arrested. Another young chap, and one whose own family had lost money in the old swindle, and that sort of confirmed it. But he refused to name his accomplices, if any, and the stolen money was not found on him. Well, the police had a couple of witnesses who identified him so the chap was found guilty, and went to the gallows.

"Masters ... and this is my real point ... Masters, who was suspected on account of a description given by these same witnesses, simply vanished. Couldn't be found anywhere. At the time, the Australian police suspected that their man, the one they'd arrested, had somehow made away with Masters, though nothing could be proved there. Then one or two of those who'd lost money in the swindle got mysterious letters ... or packages, I should say, for there was no sort of explanation in them. Just money, notes to the amount that they'd lost, or a little bit more."

"Masters making amends for the swindle, then?" asked Holmes.

"So it seemed, sir. Not all of those who'd lost money were recompensed, though ... perhaps because Masters simply didn't know who they were? Anyway, that caused a bit of a stir, for a time, then the packages stopped arriving, and the whole business just became another unexplained crime. But now ... well!"

"I see," said Holmes. "And your theory, then, is that this Cedric Masters made good his escape, came here to Singapore, and set up in business with the stolen cash, or some of it, having changed his name?"

"Is it possible, do you not think?" asked Ellis. "The one chap vanishes into thin air, the other appears from nowhere about the same time ... and then the similarity of the names, Cedric Masters and Derek Masterton. What d'you think, Mr Holmes?"

"Your account has been most interesting, Mr Ellis." Holmes frowned. "Although there are certain points which puzzle me."

"Still," Ingham interjected, "it does rather cast a cloud over Mr Masterton, does it not?"

"Oh, I agree. I think that we must by all means have a word with Mr Derek Masterton," said Holmes.

I groaned aloud. "But not right now, surely," I protested.

Holmes glanced at his watch. "You are quite right, as always, Watson," he said.

I gave a great gasp of relief. "Thank ..."

"We must first take a look at the room in which Mrs Gerard was poisoned. Let us hope that not too much has been disarranged."

"Holmes, I really must ..."

"Thank you, Mr Ellis," said Holmes, rising to his feet and shaking the private investigator's rather podgy hand. "I shall be in touch, never fear. Come along Watson. Superintendent, did you wish to take another look at the scene of the crime?"

Superintendent Ingham smiled tolerantly. "If you like, Mr Holmes. See you later, Harry," he told Ellis.

As Holmes strode out into the crowded street, he told Ingham, "I am really very glad that you have decided to come along, Superintendent."

"It's good of you to say so, sir," replied Ingham, flattered.

"Because, in all the excitement, I quite forgot to make a note of the address of the Gerards' lodgings."

"Ah." Ingham thought about this for a moment, then smiled at me. "A warranted cure for big-headedness, is Mr Holmes."

"That he is," I said.

Ingham, no doubt put out by Holmes' rudeness, looked round and hailed a carriage, and in a very short time we were rattling through streets which were unfamiliar to me, and by no means as impressive as the ones I had seen up to now.

The streets were no less crowded, though it was approaching the hour for dinner. Indeed, if anything the crowds seemed to have increased, perhaps because little stalls were appearing here and there, offering the equivalent of a seven-course banquet for a few pence. The aromas from these served to remind me that I had not yet dined, and that I had no notion as to when that happy event might occur. To keep my mind off thoughts of food, I asked Holmes, "What did you mean about having doubts as to Mr Ellis's tale? What puzzles you about it?"

"Well, Watson, the man whom Mr Ellis described seemed almost like a modern Robin Hood, robbing the rich to repay the poor victims of a swindle. Would such an altruist kill a woman?"

"H'mm. But if that woman seemed to threaten his liberty? His life, indeed? For he will pay with his life if he is a murderer, Holmes."

Holmes nodded, in silence, but looked far from satisfied.

The carriage stopped before a very ordinary sort of building, three storeys, in need of a lick of paint, and with a hand-written sign in one window advertising rooms to let. The place stood on a corner formed by the road and a little alley which ran down one side, and which did not seem to me the sort of little alley I should care to wander down alone on a dark night. It was not a very prepossessing establishment that the Gerards had patronized, I thought as I followed Holmes and Ingham to the front door.

A middle-aged woman, with the same air of dowdiness that characterized the outside of the building, emerged from the shadows as we entered the place. "Gentlemen?" she began, and then, catching sight of Ingham, "Oh, it's you, Superintendent. I thought you might return, sir, to take a look at the rooms, or ask questions or something."

"Indeed," said Holmes, his face lighting up. "Then the rooms have not been cleaned at all?"

"No, sir," said the landlady. "I left them just as they were when … you know. I thought it as well not to move anything, just in case. And besides, the maids are a bit nervous about going in there."

"Excellent," said Holmes, rubbing his hands together. "Madam, you have restored my faith in humanity."

The landlady smiled at this, looking considerably less anxious than she had at the outset of our conversation. "Can you find your way, Superintendent, or shall I …"

"No need, madam, I remember the room. Do you have the key? Thank you." And off went Ingham, striding up the stairs two at a time.

He paused at a door on the second floor. "Here we are." He opened the door, and stood back to let us enter.

I followed Holmes into the room. It was plainly furnished as a sitting room and quite clean. It bore the customary traces of recent occupancy, a book on the table, a bottle of brandy and some glass bottles of soda water on a sideboard. "Bedroom through there?" said Holmes, and set off into the other room. "Where was the body?" he called back over his shoulder.

"In this little sitting room, sir," replied Ingham. "Slumped over the table here."

"And the box of poisoned sweets?"

"On the table as well."

Holmes subjected the place to his usual thorough examination, scurrying here and there and emitting an occasional grunt as he thought he found something out of the ordinary. When he had done, he looked ruefully at Ingham.

"Well, Superintendent, you did say there was nothing here worth seeing."

Ingham nodded. "Without boasting, I think I'd have spotted anything untoward, Mr Holmes. Still, nothing like a first-hand demonstration, is there?"

"Indeed not. Well, a quick word with the landlady, and we can think about our dinner."

"Thank Heavens for that," I told myself, as I followed Holmes back down the stairs.

The landlady, evidently alerted by some mysterious sixth sense, appeared as we descended into the reception area. "Everything satisfactory, gentlemen?" she asked.

"Most satisfactory, madam," Holmes replied. He glanced around him. "You have the telephone, I observe?"

"The guests expect it these days, sir, even in a modest establishment such as mine."

"And it was you who called the police yesterday, after ... when the tragedy occurred?"

"It was, sir. Poor Mr Gerard was in such a taking, as was only natural, poor man, him having just found his poor wife in that shocking fashion."

"Dreadful, indeed, and understandable, of course," agreed Holmes in his most soothing tones. He looked round the little corridor once again. "But, as I understand it, Mr Gerard did not at once ask you to call the police? He himself went out into the street, to begin with?"

"Yes, sir, that's right. Poor Mr Gerard came racing down the stairs, and he shouted something at me ... I couldn't say what it was, not to save my life ... and then he rushed out into the street there. He was back at once, though, and said 'There's been a dreadful accident. Can you telephone to the police at once?' and so I did."

"Yes, I see. Mr Gerard went out there, presumably he looked for a policeman and failed to see one, and then he came straight back in here." Holmes nodded, then smiled at the landlady. "Thank you, madam, that is very clear. We'll bother you no longer, so good evening to you." And he nodded to Ingham and me to indicate that we should leave.

Just outside the door, Holmes halted on the pavement. He looked round, then smiled. "As I thought."

"Holmes?"

Holmes nodded down the road, by way of answer. The road on which the apartment house stood was not a main road, though it was still crowded with people going this way and that, all, presumably, heading for their dinner. But not fifty yards off it ran into a much busier thoroughfare, and on this corner stood a policeman, directing the traffic, which was considerable. "Would there have been a constable there yesterday?" Holmes asked Ingham.

"Yes, sir, there would," Ingham replied, his face grim.

"Which does raise an interesting question." Holmes looked round. "If Gerard did not come out here to look for a policeman ... and the fact that there was a policeman just a short way off rather suggests that he did not ... then what did he come out here for?" Holmes nodded at the little alley that ran on one side of the apartment house. "Let us take a look down here." And off he went, Ingham and I following.

As we entered the alley, a couple of very suspicious characters in very dirty rags cast us a sidelong glance as if summing up our personal wealth, then, evidently seeing in Ingham a person of authority, shuffled away rapidly. A few yards down the alley and it became positively sordid, a half dozen dustbins leaning drunkenly against the wall, their lids askew and their contents spilling on to the very roadway.

Holmes indicated these squalid containers. "Superintendent, it occurs to me that if a man desired to conceal something from the official gaze, something which he had taken from his hotel room, perhaps, but he had only a little time at his disposal, he might well dash out here upon some pretext and place this *something* in one of these dustbins."

Ingham gazed at the vile congeries in some dismay. "D'you want me to get a couple of constables to take a look, sir?"

"Well, if it becomes necessary. But let us first try to reconstruct events. He comes along the alley, sees these dustbins. He does not choose the first, for that is what any searcher would look at immediately. The second ... h'mm, full though it is, there is still enough space for an undiscriminating householder to insert yet more refuse, and that might lead to detection. The third ... ah! This is more like it, full to overflowing, and far enough away from the entrance to the alley to escape all but the most determined inspection."

He stood as far away from the dustbin as he decently could, and gingerly lifted the lid with the end of his walking stick, probing gently at the festering contents. I was just thinking that this was no way to work up an appetite for dinner, when Holmes stiffened, and darted forward. "I was right," he crowed, holding aloft a small object.

I offered him my handkerchief, to clean the object up slightly, and this he did, afterwards handing it to me. Ingham came close to me, staring over my shoulder.

The object was a tiny bottle, six-sided and of dark blue glass. It contained a white powder, and it bore the remains of a label, very grimy after its sojourn in the dustbin, but upon which could still be seen a skull and crossbones, and the legend, 'Arsenic. POISONOUS'

Chapter Eight

Charles Gerard Reconsiders

"Holmes?"

We were on our way back to the police station, and Holmes was holding the little blue poison bottle on his knee, both hands clasped around it as if it were some precious jewel. He was not looking at the bottle, though, but staring out of the carriage window, oblivious to the crowds round about.

I tapped the little bottle. "Holmes?" I said a second time.

He turned slowly, and a smile crept to the corners of his mouth. "Well, Watson? What are your thoughts on the matter?"

"It makes no sense at all," I said bluntly. "When a man poisons a box of sweetmeats in order to kill his wife, he surely doesn't leave the poison bottle lying around until the very last minute before getting rid of it."

Ingham, seated opposite me, nodded agreement. "And what's more, having at long last removed the bottle, he doesn't leave the poisonous sweeties there to be found by the police analyst."

"That's right," I said, warming to my work. "If Charles Gerard had poisoned the sweets, he would … well!"

And unable to think of anything more dazzlingly impressive, I added lamely, "He'd have made a damned sight better job of it than that. Why, even I could have made a better job of it than that!"

Holmes nodded. "You are both right, of course. Indeed, I confess that much the same thought had occurred to me. And yet ... and yet, Charles Gerard put this poison bottle in the rubbish in the alley, that it might not be discovered in the rooms. One might possibly have believed his story of looking for a policeman, had there not been a perfectly acceptable policeman not a hundred yards away. True, he may have been too distraught to think straight, but then he would have been more likely to dash off down the street tearing at his hair and gnashing his teeth. No, he must have raced down those stairs and outside for the express purpose of concealing this little bottle. Nothing else makes sense. But why? Why on earth ..." and he broke off, much as I had done a moment before, thereby making me feel considerably better. For if Holmes could make no sense of it, I could hardly be expected to do any better.

Then a thought struck me. Perhaps, just this once, I could see the solution where Holmes had entirely failed to do so? "Holmes," I said, casually, "how's this? Gerard is indeed telling the truth. He really did dash outside to look for a policeman, but, being distraught, as you put it, he failed to see the chap on duty at the road junction. Or perhaps the constable had left his post for a moment, one of the drivers may have been blocking the road or something, and so Gerard could not see him? It's the sort of thing that could be explained easily enough, under the circumstances. Anyway, suppose that someone else ... the real murderer ... had put that bottle in the dustbin?"

"And why, pray?"

"Why, to implicate Charles Gerard, of course." And I sat back in my seat, enjoying my little triumph. After all, it isn't very often that I score over Holmes.

"H'mm. It is an interesting line of thought. But then," said Holmes, a twinkle in his eye, "would it not have been just as easy ... and perhaps, indeed, more certain of success ... to have put the bottle in Charles Gerard's suitcase, or his wash bag, say, rather than in an alley where it might never be found?"

"Oh!"

Holmes patted my shoulder in a kindly, if patronizing, fashion. "Although it has flaws as a theory," he said, "I can really think of nothing better." And then, all of a sudden, he stiffened, sat rigid on his seat, and stared straight ahead with eyes that saw nothing. "Unless ..." and he stopped.

"Holmes?"

But not another word would he say, and a couple of minutes more saw us at the entrance to the police station.

* * *

"Can't a fellow have any rest at all?" complained Charles Gerard, as he sat down on the hard deal chair in the little room where Ingham had caused the prisoner to be brought. Gerard wiped the sweat from his face, for the evening was sweltering by now. "There's some drunk in the cell next to mine, and he keeps singing and cursing, and then just as I'm getting accustomed to him, I'm dragged up here for the third interview in one day ... or is it the fourth? I've quite lost count."

Without saying a word, Holmes took the little blue glass bottle from his pocket and placed it on the scarred and discoloured surface of the table. "Do you recognize this at all?" he asked quietly.

Gerard glanced at the table without thinking, and then looked quickly away. If ever I saw recognition on a man's face, I saw it in his. Recognition, aye, and guilt to boot. He could not prevent himself from flinching. He licked his lips nervously, and still avoided looking at the table.

"Perhaps if you were to study the bottle more closely, you would be able to say if you knew it or not," said Holmes gently.

With a perceptible effort, Gerard turned his head and glanced again at the little bottle. "No." It was almost a shout, but then he added, more quietly, "No, I don't believe I ever saw it before."

"And what if I said that you were seen concealing this bottle in a dustbin in the alley at the side of your lodgings? Not the first dustbin, nor the second, but the third?"

Gerard stared at Holmes, and for a moment it almost looked to me as if he were about to deny everything a second time. Then he just collapsed, not literally, but the spirit seemed to go out of him. He slumped in his chair, and for a moment I thought he was going to faint, and that my professional services might be called upon. I half rose, but Gerard looked up at me and shook his head. "No need for that, Doctor," he said, with a valiant attempt at humour. And to Holmes, he said, "Well, sir, if you have a witness, there is little use my denying it."

Ingham said, "Charles Gerard, do you admit concealing this bottle of arsenic?"

"Yes." His tone was dull, as if he saw no sort of hope for himself.

"The bottle was in your rooms?"

"Yes."

"And you used it to poison your wife, Emily Gerard?"

There was a pause here. Gerard stared at the Superintendent, as if he did not properly understand the question. Then, in a tone that was no more than a hoarse whisper, he answered, "Yes."

"And what about the poisoned sugarplums?" It was Holmes who asked this, his voice incisive.

"What?" Gerard stared at him. "Oh ... those! Oh ... well ... that is, I ..." and he ended the incoherent sentence with a shrug, as if he were well rid of it.

"And, more to the point, what about the note?" asked Holmes quietly.

If Gerard had seemed first guilty and then indifferent, he was now visibly shocked. Indeed, he almost leapt from the chair he sat in. "Note?" he stammered. "What note? What d'you mean, Mr Holmes?"

Holmes said, "If I am correct, there was a note near your wife's body, along with this bottle. Superintendent Ingham did not mention finding any note and therefore I conclude that you destroyed it. Am I right?"

Gerard shook his head, and looked away.

Ingham interjected, "Mr Gerard, you have already admitted tampering with evidence, a very serious matter. If there was further evidence which you have concealed or destroyed, it would be as well to tell us about it."

Gerard merely shook his head again.

"You see," said Holmes in a dreamy tone, "there remains the matter of the poisoned sugarplums. Can it be, Mr Gerard, that you entirely fail to see the significance of those? Or shall I explain?"

Gerard looked blankly at him. "You keep talking about poison in those damned sugarplums," he said, "but I say you are wrong there, Mr Holmes. That is, if you are right ..." and he broke off, looking even more baffled than I felt just then, if that were possible.

"It is indeed a puzzle, is it not?" said Holmes. "Because, as you have just realized, if your wife intended to commit suicide by first poisoning the sugarplums ..."

"What?" roared Ingham and I together.

Holmes completely ignored us. "... then the sole reason must have been to conceal the fact of its *being* suicide," he concluded. "And thus the bottle would not have been left in public view. Now, Mr Gerard, if I am to help you ... and I should like to do so if possible, for your complete ineptitude convinces me of your innocence ... then I can only do so if you will tell me the truth. Was there a note?"

Gerard stared at him in silence for a moment, and then nodded. "Yes," he muttered.

"And where is it now?"

"I burned it," said Gerard defiantly. "In that stinking alleyway. You'll not find it, Mr Holmes."

"It might be better if we did," said Holmes in a significant tone. "For you, that is."

"And for Emily?" Gerard stared at Holmes with something of his previous defiance, then his face changed. "But, then ... if ... that is ..."

"If your wife did not kill herself, and you did not ... yes," said Holmes. "In that event, you must certainly give us what help you can, so that we may determine who did kill her. And if I am wrong, then it will not help your wife should you hang for a crime which you did not commit."

"Yes. Yes, of course." Gerard thought about it and nodded. "You are right, of course, Mr Holmes. Yes, there was a note. But ..." and he shook his head.

"Mr Gerard? Having come this far, you might as well continue."

"I suppose so. Yes, there was a note, but it was in Emily's own handwriting."

Holmes leaned forward, an eager look on his face. "Ah! You are sure?"

"Certain."

"And do you recall what it said?"

Gerard nodded, dumbly. "How can I possibly forget, Mr Holmes? It is forever engraved upon my brain. 'Can you find it in you to forgive me?' it said. 'I really cannot help myself, my dearest one. I have never felt such emotion before, nor shall again'. That was it, Mr Holmes, word for word, I swear it."

"There was no superscription? The note was not addressed to you by name?"

Gerard shook his head. "It was exactly as I have said, Mr Holmes. Word for word, no preamble and no signature."

"But you would swear it was your wife's writing?"

"I do swear it."

"Tell me," said Holmes, "was it a whole sheet of paper?"

Gerard shook his head. "A half sheet."

"Ah! Was it torn, or had it been cut? Did you happen to notice?"

Gerard closed his eyes, as if trying to visualize the note. "The sheet had been folded and torn across the middle, as you do when you're writing a hasty memorandum or something of the sort. The note itself, the text, I mean, was written on the top half, so the fold and tearing was at the bottom of the note itself."

Holmes nodded. "Anything else? Was the paper of decent quality, say?"

"Yes. In fact, it was just the sort of notepaper upon which Emily was accustomed to write her letters to me, before our marriage." He gave a bitter, fleeting little smile. "I remember noticing the watermark, you see. And there was a faint perfume about it, for Emily sometimes used scented ink."

"I see."

Gerard frowned, as if trying to remember more. "And there was a little tear on the top, where it had been ripped from the notepad, I imagine."

"Was this tear to the left of the sheet, or the right?"

"The right."

"Was your wife left-handed?"

"No."

"Tell me, if you would, what occurred that day, when you returned to your lodgings."

"I went in, there was nobody about ... the place is usually quiet through the day. I went upstairs and called out to my wife, so that she would not be unduly concerned when the door opened."

"The door was unlocked, then?"

"Yes." Gerard went on, "I saw Emily slumped over the table. I knew at once that something was amiss, that she was not just dozing. I ran to her, saw ... saw ..."

"Yes, yes," said Holmes gently. "Then you saw the bottle, and the note?"

Gerard nodded. "The bottle was on top of the note, like some obscene paperweight. There was a glass there, too, with the remains of some brandy, and some cloudy stuff, I assumed it was the dregs of the poison that ... you know. Well, I couldn't tell you just what went through my mind right then. I guess I went mad for a short time. Then I managed to pull myself together, though I couldn't say just how I did it. I remembered the silly argument, Emily's headache that I'd thought was just an excuse not to go out with me ... I blamed myself, you see."

"For what you thought was suicide?"

"What else could I think? The glass, the bottle and the note in her very handwriting." Gerard shook his head again, as if trying to clear it. "Well, I didn't want her found like that, not with the poison there. I washed the glass and put it in the bathroom. Then I had to get rid of the note and the bottle. I picked them up and ran downstairs ... the landlady had appeared by that time, so I had to make some excuse for running outside. I shouted some nonsense or the other, went out and round the corner into the alleyway. There was nobody much about in there, despite the road in front of the place being crowded, so I put a match to the note, and shoved the bottle into one of the dustbins. That's all, I swear, Mr Holmes."

Holmes nodded. "It is much as I had imagined."

Gerard looked at my old friend, a glimmer of hope appearing for the first time in his eye. "But, Mr Holmes ... do you really see any light in this dark and tragic business?"

"It is too soon to put it in those terms just yet. I should prefer to say that I see certain inconsistencies in the matter. Inconsistencies which need further investigation, but which I hope and trust will remove the cloud of suspicion which currently hangs over you."

"I am truly grateful, sir," said Gerard quietly. "For myself, for obvious reasons, but more than that ... for Emily's sake. For I may say that on reflection I cannot believe that she committed suicide. And I can think of no man who is better qualified than Mr Sherlock Holmes to bring the truth to light. If you cannot do it, sir, nobody can."

Holmes nodded. "Thank you. One last question only, sir, and that a rather delicate one. Was your wife of an affectionate nature?"

Gerard stared at him in amazement.

"I must ask it," said Holmes.

"Well, sir, then I reply that Emily was as affectionate a wife as any reasonable man could wish," said Gerard stiffly.

"Thank you," said Holmes, nodding to the constable who stood at attention by the door.

When Gerard had been taken out of the room, Holmes sat back and looked at Ingham and me. "Well, gentlemen?"

Ingham shook his head. "It's a rum tale, and no mistake," he said slowly. "I'd be inclined to think Master Gerard was trying to fool us, but there remains the problem of the poisoned sugarplums. If he did kill his wife, why move the poison bottle, but leave the poisoned sweets?"

"And then what d'you make of the letter?" asked Holmes.

I answered, "That sounded odd, too. Of course, we have only Gerard's word that any letter existed."

"But why should he lie? He admits to concealing the bottle ... the act of a man who has not thought things through, surely? He could have denied the existence of a letter ... or, if he planned to kill his wife and make it look like suicide, why not leave the letter there? Anyway, assuming for a moment that there was such a letter as he described? What then?"

"Then, it is odd that an affectionate woman should say 'my dearest', instead of 'my dear husband'," I replied. "Or again, she spoke of some 'emotion', where one might have thought she'd say 'oppression', or 'depression', or something stronger."

"Your conclusion?"

"That the so-called *suicide note* was nothing of the kind!" I replied triumphantly. "It was a portion of a longer letter, sent to a friend, hence 'my dearest one', or whatever it was." I frowned at Holmes. "A former lover, perhaps? When she married Gerard?"

"It is possible."

"The note was faked, then. But the business about Mrs Gerard being left-handed? What was that all about?"

Holmes handed me his notebook. "You, like Mrs Gerard, are right-handed. Be so kind as to tear a sheet from my little book there."

I took the book, flipped it open, and gripped the top sheet with my right hand. "Oh! I tear from right to left, of course. And if the sheet were to stick, and a piece be left behind on the pad, it would be on the left. But then ... ah! The missing portion was a figure, '2' or '3' or something that would show at once that it was part of a longer letter. Simple, of course."

"Absurdly so," said Holmes.

"Though that still does not tell us the letter's original recipient, does it?"

"True," said Holmes, "but there is one very obvious candidate."

"The sister, you mean?" asked Ingham.

Holmes nodded.

"Yes, and it was the sister who gave Gerard the box of poisoned sugarplums," said Ingham slowly. Then he frowned. "But in that case, why leave the sweetmeats to be found? And, if she were wanting to kill her sister with the sweetmeats, why the nonsense with the bottle and note?" He shook his head. "I'm floundering, I'm afraid. Any ideas, Mr Holmes, Doctor Watson?"

"Perhaps two separate people wanted her dead?" I suggested tentatively ... silly, I know, but it was the only thing that might have made some sort of sense to me.

Holmes treated the suggestion as it richly deserved. He made a noise indicative of disbelief. "In that event, the late Mrs Gerard must have been more unpopular than is usual in one so young."

"Well, let's hear your brilliant proposition, Holmes."

Holmes took out his pipe and filled it slowly. "It is a puzzle, I agree. But how's this? The sister plans to kill Mrs Gerard, but make it look like suicide ... why, we cannot yet imagine. She knows of her sister's fondness for walnut confectionery, and doctors the appropriate sweets, sending them via the husband. Mrs Gerard eats the four walnut-centred sweets, dies, and the sister comes into the room and leaves the bottle, note and glass. How's that?"

"Possible," I said doubtfully.

"But?"

"But ... it leaves a lot to chance, Holmes. A lot unexplained."

"And I agree there, too," he said thoughtfully. "And yet the presence of poison in the sugarplums is somehow related to the death of Mrs Gerard. It must be so, or it would be the most enormous coincidence yet."

Superintendent Ingham stood up. "Well," said he, "I don't know about you gents, but I'm ready for my dinner."

"Me, too," I said.

Holmes laughed. "I might as well make it unanimous."

"You gentlemen will be my guests at the Raffles Hotel," said Ingham. I promise you, you're in for a treat. But I'll tell you this," he added, as he led the way outside, "first thing tomorrow, I'm having a few words with Mrs Masterton, despite what the doctors may say."

"And with Mr Masterton too, perhaps?" suggested Holmes.

Ingham nodded. "Whatever the rights and wrongs of it, the Mastertons have some explaining to do."

Chapter Nine

Mrs Masterton Explains ...

"A grand morning, Holmes."

Holmes gave a grunt that might have meant anything, and continued to gaze out of the carriage window. Superintendent Ingham had been as good as his word and bought us dinner the previous night at the Raffles Hotel; and the food had been every bit as good as he had boasted. I had enjoyed my meal, but Holmes – as was his way when engaged upon a case – had failed to do proper justice to what was before him, and more than once had the anxious waiter asked him if all was well, to be answered with a wan smile. Ingham, too, had been concerned about my old friend, but I assured the Superintendent that there was nothing that need worry him and that it was merely Holmes' custom. After dinner Holmes had retired early, saying that he needed to think in peace. Ingham and I had treated ourselves to a few gin concoctions at the bar – a few too many in my own case, I regret to say. And then I had sought my bed, and knew nothing more until the tropical sun streaming through my window caused me to awaken.

A magnificent breakfast started the day properly – for me, at any rate, though Holmes' own meal was rather frugal, I regret to say – and now we were rolling along the busy streets heading for the Masterton house. It was marginally cooler than it had been on the previous night, but I knew that the day would quickly become uncomfortably hot.

Superintendent Ingham packed some evil-smelling tobacco into his pipe, drew air through it experimentally, adjusted the density of the filling to his satisfaction, and applied a match. Through a cloud of blue smoke, he asked, "Solved it, Mr Holmes?"

Holmes turned his gaze from the bustle around us, and smiled. "I have a half dozen theories," he told Ingham, "of which three are significant, and all would serve to explain part of the mystery. The trouble is that none will serve to explain it all. We need more to work on, I fear."

"Well, let's just hope that Anya and Derek Masterton will provide it," said Ingham, and we lapsed into a silence that continued until the carriage halted outside the Masterton house.

The house was low, new and smart, and set in its own grounds in what Ingham told us was the most fashionable area of the city. The grounds were bright with flowers and trees, the work of several skilled local gardeners, as I judged. It was all in strong contrast to the rather dowdy lodging house which the Gerards had favoured, and I could not help but wonder just why Charles Gerard had been so insistent on their not staying here with their relatives. Suspicious, that, surely? But then, if Charles Gerard had wanted privacy in order to murder his wife, why had he not ordered matters better? I mentally shrugged my shoulders, gave it up, and got down from the carriage to follow Ingham and Holmes to the front door.

The door was opened by a butler who would not have been at all out of place in Mayfair or Belgravia, and who sedately ushered us into a large and airy drawing room. "Mrs Masterton is awake and feeling a little better," he told us in answer to Ingham's enquiry, "and I shall find out if she will see you gentlemen." And off he went, solemn as before.

Holmes glanced round the room. "It is an impressive house," he said.

Ingham nodded. "Masterton has done well for himself these past few years, and no mistake."

"He thus has much to lose, then, should there be some murky secret in his past?" mused Holmes.

"That he has," said Ingham, with another nod.

Further speculation was prevented by the entrance of Mr and Mrs Masterton. Derek Masterton was some six feet tall, forty years of age or perhaps just a trifle more, with his wavy hair just beginning to go grey and his moustache neatly clipped. He wore a beautifully tailored lightweight suit in a pearl grey material, and, in short, he looked every inch the successful businessman. Mrs Masterton was some ten years younger than her husband, strikingly attractive, but with the strain of the last day or two showing only too clearly upon her face. She entered the room leaning on her husband's arm, and he escorted her to a chair.

When the necessary introductions had been made, Ingham told Derek Masterton, "We'd like a word with Mrs Masterton first, if you could excuse us, sir?"

Masterton frowned. "I'm not sure that I can allow that," he said, his tone firm but not belligerent. "My wife has had a tremendous shock, you know, and has not been at all well. Indeed, the doctor has expressly forbidden any excitement for a time. Can you not ask me your questions? I'll answer as fully and as honestly as I can. Or at any rate, let me stay here while you talk to Anya."

"It's the form, Mr Masterton," replied Ingham, his voice every bit as courteous, but every bit as uncompromising, as Masterton's own. "We'll need to talk to you too, of course, but if we could speak to Mrs Masterton first, and then she can get back to her rest?"

"Well, could Miss Earnshaw not remain here in the room, at least?"

"And we'll perhaps have a quick word with Miss Earnshaw, as well, later on," said Ingham. He smiled at Masterton. "There's no need to worry about there being someone here to see fair play, sir. We're all quite civilized, you know." And he added to Mrs Masterton, "Merely a matter of routine, madam. You'll want to help us clear up the tragic matter of your sister's death, now won't you?"

Masterton clearly did not like it; but equally clearly Ingham was not going to give way. So, with a muttered, "Have it your own way," Derek Masterton cast one last look at Ingham, another at his wife, and reluctantly showed himself out.

"Now, Mrs Masterton," Ingham began, "I'm not sure just how much you already know concerning the circumstances of your unfortunate sister's demise."

Anya Masterton put a tiny lace handkerchief to her face. "I know that poor Emily is dead, of course," she said. "And Derek hinted that there was some ... some doubt ... some suspicion ... as to the cause of her death. Oh, but he must be wrong," she added in a stronger tone. "Surely it is enough that poor Emily has been taken from me, without there being any hint of ... no! It is madness to think it."

Ingham, embarrassed, cleared his throat. "I'm afraid your husband is quite right, though, Mrs Masterton. I wish it were otherwise, and I wish there was an easier way to tell you this, but the plain fact is that Mrs Gerard was poisoned."

"Oh!"

I rose to my feet as Mrs Masterton seemed to shrink into the chair, but she waved me away. "No need, thank you, Doctor Watson, I am not the fainting type," she told me. And to Ingham, she said, "You are sure?"

"Quite sure, madam. Again, I wish we weren't."

"I see. And I believe that you have arrested Charles ... Mr Gerard, that is?"

Ingham nodded.

Mrs Masterton shook her head in disbelief. "It is ridiculous. I'm sure you must have some reason ... what you think of as good reason ... for suspecting Charles, but I assure you that you are wrong."

Holmes stirred. "There are certain discrepancies which might show that Mr Gerard is innocent," he said.

"There you are, then. Some tragic accident ... assuming, that is, that it was not some sudden illness, or ..."

"There was no possibility of accident or illness, Mrs Masterton," said Ingham heavily. "I wish there were. No, it was poison all right."

"But there are many questions left unanswered," added Holmes.

"And you think that I know the answers?" Mrs Masterton's tone was scornful.

"You may well be able to clear up some puzzling little points, madam," said Holmes.

"Very well, though I warn you that I am not very likely to be of help to your investigations."

"First of all, then," said Ingham, "can you think of anyone who might have wanted your sister dead? Anyone with a grudge against her, that sort of thing?"

"Not at all," said Mrs Masterton, shaking her head. "And if there were anyone of that kind in the whole wide world, there could surely be no-one here in Singapore, for poor Emily had never been here before. She arrived here only a day or two ago, for the first time in her life, and she knew nobody here apart from Derek and myself."

"And Miss Earnshaw, as I understand?" murmured Holmes.

"Maggie? Oh, yes, I think they knew each other vaguely in London, but were not particular friends. Not close enough to be enemies, I mean."

"I understand. Well, then," said Holmes, "did your sister ever suffer from melancholy, or depression?"

"Not in the least. Emily was of a most robust disposition, mentally as well as physically." Mrs Masterton managed a weak smile. "In fact, she had very positive views on many subjects, and hated to be shown to be in the wrong."

"Ah! There had been, I believe, a quarrel of some sort between the Gerards on the day of her death?"

For a moment, Mrs Masterton was taken aback. She sat up straight, and stared at Holmes. Then, "No," she told him, "I cannot believe that a silly quarrel would affect either my sister or her husband to any great extent ... certainly not to the extent which you appear to suggest, Mr Holmes."

Holmes raised a hand. "I suggest nothing, madam," he said. "But Mr Gerard has refused to tell us the cause of the quarrel. Perhaps you might enlighten us?"

"If I knew, Mr Holmes, I should not tell you," replied Mrs Masterton, with a little flounce of the head. "In the event, it is academic, as I do *not* know. Charles did seem on edge when he called upon us, and when my husband had gone out on business I pressed Charles as to the reason for his odd behaviour, and for Emily's failure to visit us. He admitted that there had been a minor tiff, but would not elaborate, and I did not feel inclined to press him."

"No, of course not. But to return to my line of questioning," said Holmes, "there was never anything that might have caused you to think that your sister might ever ... make away with herself?"

"Suicide?" The scorn was palpable in Mrs Masterton's voice. "I never heard such rubbish in all my life, Mr Holmes. Emily would never consider such a thing."

It was now Holmes, who was momentarily taken aback by this vehemence, recovered his composure and smiled. "That confirms my own deductions, madam. I am sorry to have to ask such things, but there is good reason, I assure you. Now, Mr Gerard has told us that he asked his new wife to make a rather peculiar will immediately after the marriage, whereby she left her own money to you, and not to her husband."

Mrs Masterton nodded, but said nothing.

"Did you know of this will?" asked Holmes.

"Oh, yes. Emily wrote and told me."

"And what did you think about it?"

Mrs Masterton considered. "I must say that I certainly thought it a little odd," she said at last. "After all, if Charles Gerard were genuinely in love with Emily, if he were not just after her money, then why should he need to prove the fact, to underline it, as it were, by asking her to leave her money to me? On the other hand, if he were truly an independent sort of man, then it might make some sense to act as he did." The wan little smile flickered briefly across her face a second time. "In either event, Mr Holmes, it seemed to me, odd though it might be, that there was no harm done by it. Not at that stage, though if Charles had later persuaded, or attempted to persuade, Emily to alter her will, I might have taken a more serious interest in the matter." She smiled once more. "And again, in either event, it does rather tend to prove Charles is innocent of Emily's murder, does it not? If he were after her money alone, then he would make very sure that her will left it to him, and not to me, before he administered poison or anything else."

"That point had occurred to me," admitted Holmes. "But tell me, having thought that the will was a trifle odd, will you now abide by its contents? Will you take your inheritance?"

"Oh, yes. It was Charles's wish that Emily make her will in that fashion ... he can hardly complain now can he? If ... when, rather ... when he is cleared of this nonsensical charge, I am sure Derek will take him into the firm, and equally sure that he will do well. And, should he later decide to set up in business on his own account, I shall happily lend, or even give, him some cash to help out. If the necessity arises, that is, for I think he has real ability, and only needs a chance to make something of himself."

"You are probably right," said Holmes unctuously. "The provisions of your own will ... forgive me ... but they are quite conventional?"

"Oh, yes. My modest fortune goes to Derek, or to the children should he predecease me. And, in case you wondered, Mr Holmes, Derek's will leaves all to me, or again to the children should I leave him first."

"You have no other family to be considered?"

"Emily was my only living relative, and Derek, poor man, had nobody either. We are quite self-contained, the two of us, and our dear children."

"Tell me, did your husband also know of the provisions of your sister's will?"

"Oh, yes. I talked about it with him, when my sister wrote to me."

"And did Miss Earnshaw know about it?"

"Yes. Miss Earnshaw is a trusted friend and confidant as well as our children's governess. Why do you ask that?"

Holmes ignored the question. "Did you correspond regularly with your sister?"

"Fairly regularly. One always wishes one had done more, said more, kept in touch on a regular basis, do you not find?"

"Yes, indeed. Tell me, did you entirely approve of your sister's marriage?"

The abruptness of the question seemed to take Mrs Masterton aback slightly. She considered a moment, then replied, "I cannot say that I approved or disapproved. Remember that I had only met Charles Gerard for the first time a week ago, or less. I was, perhaps, a little displeased as to the manner of her marriage. I felt, to be plain, that they could have waited, for Derek and I would have liked to go to England and be present at the ceremony, rather than being presented with a *fait accompli*, but that did not cause any serious rift."

"Did your sister perhaps write to you apologizing for her failure to invite you?"

"She did, as a matter of fact."

"Do you recall the words or phrases she used?"

"Not word for word," said Mrs Masterton. "She apologized for not inviting us, said that they had acted in haste out of love, the usual sort of thing."

"And do you have the letter still?"

"I do not think so. I am not particularly sentimental with regard to correspondence."

"Can you recall whether your sister ever referred to you in her letters as 'my dearest one'?"

Mrs Masterton shook her head. "Not that I remember. She usually called me by name, and I did the same. Occasionally we might have written 'my dear sister', or something of the kind, but we were generally not overly demonstrative, in the way that some people are." She regarded Holmes curiously. "Why do you ask these questions, Mr Holmes?"

"Oh, one must get to know the background, you know," said Holmes vaguely, "and hope that something emerges, as it were, from the fog. I believe that Charles Gerard gave his wife a box of sugarplums on the day of her death? Sugarplums that you in turn had given to him?"

"What an odd question. Yes, when he burbled on about a quarrel, I suggested he buy Emily a present, a peace offering, so to speak. He just sat there looking remarkably like a shorn sheep ... men are absolutely hopeless when it comes to presents for ladies. Anyway, I remembered that I had a box of sweets, a local speciality, in the house, and gave them to Charles to give to Emily." She frowned. "But you're not suggesting that there was poison in those, I hope? For if you were ..."

Holmes held up a hand. "Your sister was, I believe, particularly fond of walnut confections?"

"Mr Holmes, you are beginning to disturb me. I ..."

"Was your sister fond of walnut centres, Mrs Masterton?"

"She was."

"And you yourself?"

"Walnuts? No, I detest them. But ..."

"Do you have any preference at all in that line?"

"Mr Holmes ..."

"If you please, Mrs Masterton." It was Ingham who said this, with all the gravity he could muster.

"Oh, what nonsense. Yes, if you must know, I have a particular weakness for 'Violet Cremes', and that sort of thing."

Holmes asked, his voice quivering with suppressed excitement, "When did you buy the sugarplums, Mrs Masterton?"

"I did not. They were a present from Derek. Mr Masterton. He bought them the day before I gave them to Charles ... I knew he would not mind my giving them away, under the circumstances. Now, I really must ask, why are you asking this? Do you seriously think the sugarplums were poisoned?"

"We know they were, madam," said Ingham heavily.

"Not all of them, though," added Holmes. "The walnut centres had all been eaten, presumably by Mrs Gerard, but of those that remained, there was arsenic only in the 'Violet Cremes'."

For a moment, Mrs Masterton sat there in silence, gazing at my friend. Then she seemed to collapse inwards upon herself, and this time my professional services were needed, as she slumped to the floor in a dead faint.

Chapter Ten

... But Mr Masterton Does Not

"Damnable!" said Derek Masterton. His nostrils flared like those of some wild beast, and he drew in his breath, evidently in preparation for delivering a more elaborate condemnation. Between us we had escorted Mrs Masterton back to her bed, and she was now being fussed over – that is, being attended to – by her Chinese maid. Mr Masterton had appeared mysteriously when his wife collapsed. He had helped us get her to bed, then ushered us back downstairs, and now he was all too evidently just about to express his opinion of our methods of interrogation.

Superintendent Ingham held up a large hand. "I apologize unreservedly, sir, for any distress we may have caused your wife," he said. "But I think you'll agree that this whole business might reasonably be described as *damnable*, and so the sooner we get to the bottom of it, the better for all of us. After all, you don't shoot the messenger because the message is unwelcome do you?"

Derek Masterton considered this for a moment, then he smiled and held his hand out to the Superintendent, who shook it solemnly.

"I should apologize to you, of course," said Masterton. "But, under the circumstances, I think you'll agree that it was understandable, if not excusable? Come back into the drawing room, though, and let's sit down, for I believe you wanted to talk to me? I don't know about you chaps," he added, as we found chairs, "but I could do with a drink."

"Oh, certainly," I said. "Capital notion. Brandy, if it's all the same to you."

Holmes frowned at me, and the Superintendent made great play of being *on duty* – foolishly, in my view, for how better to lull a suspect into a false sense of security than to have a drink with him? Anyway, such was the thought in my own mind, and I happily accepted the generous measure that Derek Masterton poured for me.

"A cigar?" he said. "Please smoke your pipes, if you prefer."

"Thank you." Holmes and Ingham found their pipes, while I took a respectable cigar, which Masterton told me was from Sumatra, from a silver box.

Masterton took his time cutting and lighting his cigar, regarding the rest of us over it as he did so. Playing for time, perhaps? I had the distinct impression that such was the case. When the cigar was going to his satisfaction, Masterton asked, "Tell me, Mr Holmes, just what was it that so upset Anya? I can understand that the whole thing has been a bit of a shock to her, naturally, but she seemed to be getting over the worst, and now ... this."

"It was the shock of hearing the details, I think, sir," said Ingham.

"Ah, yes, the details," said Masterton. "You've played it very close to your chest, Superintendent, with regard to the details. I take it you're going to let me into the secret, too, now?"

"We've been deliberately cagey, sir," replied Ingham stolidly. "The fewer people who get to know the details at this stage, the better it is for us, the police."

Masterton thought about this. "Oh, I see. If someone lets slip they know a bit too much, then you can ask 'em just how come they know, is that it?"

"That's it exactly, sir." Ingham kept his voice level, but I knew that he was thinking the same as I was, namely that Mr Derek Masterton knew a little too much about police procedures for comfort. Holmes, of course, would have worked that out at first glance from the state of Masterton's shoes, or something equally improbable. Ingham went on, "Now, I believe that you bought a box of these 'Singapore Sugarplums' for Mrs Masterton recently? Is that so?"

Masterton looked at him blankly. "No. But what on earth ..."

"Are you quite sure you didn't buy a box of that particular confectionery, sir?"

Masterton seemed about to protest, then he gave little start. "Oh. Now you mention it, I think I did buy Anya a box of the damned things, but that was a day or so ago. I'd quite forgotten."

"Is that so, sir? Tell me, does Mrs Masterton have a special liking for those sugarplums?" asked Ingham.

Masterton shrugged his shoulders. "Not really. She eats one now and then. Though she does have a taste for 'Violet Cremes', she normally eats those right off."

"But not this time?" Holmes suggested.

Another shrug. "Didn't she? I couldn't tell you." Masterton regarded us closely. "From all these questions about a box of sweets, I gather that there was ... oh!" He shook his head. "But you cannot be suggesting that they were poisoned, or something? And anyway, how could a box of sweets that I'd bought for Anya possibly poison her sister?"

"We think they did, though, sir," said Ingham.

Masterton shook his head. "Out of the question."

"Mrs Masterton apparently gave the box of sweets ... untouched ... to Mr Charles Gerard, to give to his wife."

"I don't believe it. I don't believe any of it!"

"It's true, sir, or at any rate we're sure that your wife gave the sugarplums to Mr Gerard. Unless, that is, both Mr Gerard and your wife are ... are not exactly telling us the truth," said Ingham.

Masterton shook his head again in disbelief. "I cannot comprehend it," he said. "But, while I cannot speak for Charles Gerard because I have known him only a very few days ... although I have never had any reason to doubt his honesty ... I can certainly tell you that my wife would never lie to the police. If she tells you ... as you now tell me ... that she gave the box of sugarplums, which I had given her, to Charles Gerard, then I know it is so."

"Thank you, sir," said Ingham with a little nod of satisfaction.

"But that still doesn't mean that I accept for one moment that there was poison in the sugarplums."

"The police analyst found it there, sir. Arsenic."

"Good Heavens!" Masterton dropped his cigar in his agitation, and I went over and picked it up, as he seemed not to have noticed. "Thank you, Doctor Watson," he muttered in an abstracted fashion. "Well, Superintendent, gentlemen. This has come as a shock, and no mistake. Yes, I can see now why poor Anya was so taken aback by your news. But tell me, are you sure it was the same box? There is no possibility that another, poisoned, box somehow found its way to the unfortunate lady?"

"I don't think that's very likely at all, sir," said Ingham. "And that being the case, our task resolves itself into the little matter of finding out who put the poison into the sugarplums."

"Well, it wasn't me. I promise you that. And it wasn't Anya, or Miss Earnshaw."

"What about the servants? The butler?" asked Holmes.

"Good Lord, you don't suggest that the butler did it! Why, even Doctor Watson here would not use such a hackneyed device in one of his lurid tales."

"Really, sir, " I protested, my ire being intensified by hearing Holmes mumble something like, "I wouldn't be so certain."

"I'm sorry, Doctor," said Masterton with a rather forced laugh, "but the whole idea is preposterous. Anyway, isn't poison supposed to be a woman's weapon?"

"A common misconception," said Holmes smoothly. "Some of the most notorious poisoners have been men, and men of robustly masculine appetites at that, in many instances."

"H'mm." Masterton shook his head. "No, you're wrong. See here, Mr Holmes, Superintendent, if that box of sugarplums was the one I'd bought, it was never meddled with in this house. I'll stake my reputation on that."

"And your life?" asked Holmes quickly.

"What's that?"

"Consider this ... had your wife not given that box away, who would have eaten the sweets in it?"

The colour drained from Masterton's face. "Good Lord! This is getting ridiculous, Mr Holmes." He turned to me. "Doctor, you're a man whose reputation goes before you. Was that box of sugarplums really poisoned?"

"According to Doctor Oong, the police analyst, and there is no reason to suppose that he is incorrect."

"So someone really did poison the sweets?" Masterton shook his head yet again. If he were lying, he was one of the finest actors I have ever seen, on stage or off.

"Not all," said Holmes smoothly.

"How d'you mean?"

"Well, there was arsenic in four of the sweets which were uneaten, all 'Violet Cremes'."

"That makes no sense at all. Emily Gerard hated 'Violet Cremes'."

"You knew that? Yes, you clearly know. How?"

"Common knowledge. Or at any rate it was ... is ... common knowledge with us here. My wife told me, we made a joke of it. But ... wait a moment ..." Masterton put a hand to his brow. "'Violet Cremes'? Those are *my* wife's favourites. But ... then ... can it be ..."

"That someone planned to kill your wife? It is a sobering thought, is it not?" said Holmes, his tone considerably less smooth this time.

"No. But ... I simply don't understand, Mr Holmes. If the poison was in sweets which Emily Gerard hated, and were left uneaten, then how was she poisoned?"

"We suspect that there was arsenic in four other sweets, all with walnut centres."

"Oh."

"Did you know of Mrs Gerard's preference for walnuts?"

"Yes, of course. As I told you, it was a joke with us ... like Jack Sprat and his wife."

"Let us explore this *humorous* aspect further," said Holmes. "If the box had not been given away, who would have eaten the walnut centres?"

"Well, I suppose I would. Oh."

Holmes nodded. "You see the implication, Mr Masterton? There was poison in the sweets that your wife was sure to eat, and also in the ones that, in the ordinary way, she would leave untouched for you to eat. Intriguing, is it not?"

"Good Lord! Intriguing, Mr Holmes? It's terrifying." Masterton thought about it for a moment. "And then ... the children. We don't encourage them to eat sweets, they're too young, too little, but sometimes, for a treat ... great heavens! When I think ..." and he broke off with something like a sob, and mopped his brow.

"It is a dreadful business, to be sure," said Holmes.

"Dreadful indeed," agreed Masterton. "But it still makes no sense at all, sir. Why, neither Anya nor I has an enemy in the whole world."

"You are sure of that?"

"As sure as any man can be, Mr Holmes. Oh, I may have brushed men up the wrong way now and then in business, but nothing to justify this sort of thing."

"And your wife?"

"Even less need to worry about enemies than I have."

"No little ... ah, differences of opinion with any of the other ladies here?"

"Lord, no. We're a fairly tight-knit community, and the ladies, I regret to say, are the most tight-knit of all. They might well join forces against an outsider, or someone they considered an outsider, but they would never quarrel amongst themselves."

"And would they have regarded Mrs Gerard as *an outsider*, d'you think?" asked Holmes quickly.

Masterton laughed, but there was no humour in it. "You have a way of taking a fellow up, Mr Holmes, and pouncing on any little slip of the tongue. No, I think that Emily Gerard, had she lived and remained here, would have fitted into our little circle very nicely."

"You yourself seem to have *fitted in* very well since your arrival in Singapore, which was, so I understand, not that very long ago?" said Holmes.

"Oh, it's a few years now," said Masterton easily.

"And what were you doing before you arrived here?" asked Holmes. "No-one seems to know precisely."

Masterton retrieved his cigar from the ashtray where I had placed it, took an experimental puff, and applied another match, taking the same care over lighting it as he had done originally, while considering Holmes' question – and perhaps his own reply – while he did so. At length he said, "Out here, 'East of Suez', Mr Holmes, a man's past isn't always what it might have been had he remained all his life in London. And it isn't really considered good form to enquire too deeply, if you follow me."

"Indeed I do."

"I will say this," added Masterton, "there is nothing, and nobody, in my past that would account for any animosity leading to murder. Will that satisfy you? There is a Bible somewhere in the house, should you want me to take my oath."

"That is not necessary. But let us return to this famous box of sugarplums," said Holmes, with only a tinge of exasperation audible in his voice. "You say that you bought them a few days ago?"

"I did buy them a few days ago."

"Can you remember the day more precisely?"

"I'm not sure I can. It isn't the sort of thing a man does remember, is it?" Masterton frowned. "Wait a minute, though. Yes, it was Monday. That is, I'm pretty certain it was Monday."

"The day on which the Gerards arrived in Singapore, that is to say?"

136

"Yes, it was. Or at least I believe it was, for as I say, I cannot swear to it. But if it was Monday, then it was merely a chronological coincidence, Mr Holmes, and nothing more sinister."

"Was there any particular reason for your buying the box of sugarplums?"

"Nothing special. I had been absent from the office for the weekend, of course, then on my way home on the Monday ... yes, it was Monday, of course it was ... I chanced to pass a little tobacconist and confectioner's shop, I buy my own tobacco there, as a matter of fact. I stopped to buy a couple of ounces of my usual mixture, then I noticed the box in the window, and thought I'd bring Anya a little present. No special occasion, you know ... if it had been a birthday or a wedding anniversary I'd have bought jewellery or a silk nightgown, something of that sort. Wish I had, now." He shrugged. "No, nothing special. Just a sort of spur of the moment thing, it might have been flowers, but this time it was a box of sugarplums."

"So that was definitely on the Monday? And Mrs Masterton passed the box to Charles Gerard on Thursday. That is four days," said Holmes. He smiled at Masterton. "In my experience, it is unusual for a box of sweets to remain so long about the place unopened."

Masterton shrugged again. "Neither of us has what is called 'a sweet tooth'."

"And yet you bought a box of sugarplums, rather than that bunch of flowers, which you might have bought?"

"I have told you, Mr Holmes, it was ..."

"*A spur of the moment thing*, yes, I know."

Masterton's face flushed, and he half rose from his chair. By my side Ingham tensed his body, but Masterton sat back with a weak laugh. "Yes, that's it exactly, Mr Holmes."

"Now, were you aware that Mrs Gerard had made a will leaving her money to her sister, your wife?"

"Yes, of course. Anya told me. I thought it a bit odd, but I could do nothing about it, and probably wouldn't if I could. It was Emily's own money, after all, and she was old enough to leave it where she wished."

"And on a related topic, your wife has made a will leaving all her money to you?"

Masterton flushed again.

"Forgive me," said Holmes, "but I am desperately trying to make some sense of all this by determining who may have stood to gain from it all."

"Well, my wife gains by Emily's will, which rather lets Charles Gerard out, unless he had some other reason to kill his wife," said Masterton. "As for poison in the sweetmeats meant for my wife … assuming for one moment that there's any truth in that ridiculous nonsense … then I'm the only one who stood to gain there. And I can only repeat, I didn't attempt to poison my wife, though I don't suppose it's any use saying it."

"I accuse you of nothing," said Holmes, holding up a hand. "But tell me this, Mr Masterton, if you and your wife had unfortunately succumbed to that box of poisoned sugarplums, then who would gain from such a double tragedy?"

"The children, of course. If you can call it *gaining* to lose both parents."

"But they are not of age? Too young to handle a large fortune?"

"Just so … and too young to doctor a box of sweets," added Masterton with some contempt in his voice.

"Just so," repeated Holmes. "Mrs Masterton has, I believe, no family apart from her late sister?"

"That's right."

"And you?"

"I have no family living," said Masterton.

"I am sorry to hear it. So who would have control of the money, until the children came of age? Miss Earnshaw, perhaps?"

"Maggie Earnshaw? Good Lord, no." Masterton laughed at this. "No, the money would go into trust, and the children into the care of a pal of mine, Tommy Wharton. He and his wife have two boys of their own, but slightly older than our two, so there would be no difficulty there. As a matter of fact, Tommy has made a will leaving his children to me, in the event that his only relative, his brother, should not be living if Tommy and Mrs Wharton both ... you know."

"An admirable arrangement. And this Mr Wharton is a businessman?"

"And a successful one."

"And he would have control of the capital?"

"No, of the interest only. His idea, not mine, and his will has exactly the same provision. The capital would be safe, looked after by the oldest firm of solicitors in Singapore."

"H'mm."

"Not what you expected, Mr Holmes?" asked Masterton, with a look that avoided being a sneer, but only just.

"Oh, I merely explore the possibilities," said Holmes. He said it easily enough, but he looked baffled none the less.

"And for good measure," Masterton continued, "old Tommy couldn't have doctored the sugarplums if he wanted to, because his children have the measles at the moment, and he rang me to say that I should keep well away from him for a week or so unless I wanted mine to catch the wretched things. He hasn't been to the house for a week or more, so he simply couldn't, even if he wanted to."

"I see. That is certainly conclusive. But apart from the blameless Mr Wharton, anyone who came to the house might have tampered with the box?"

"Only if they had access to my wife's boudoir, and as her husband I don't exactly encourage that, you understand."

"Miss Earnshaw would, I imagine, look in there on occasion?"

"Look here, Mr Holmes, if it's Maggie Earnshaw you've got in mind, you can forget it. I've told you that if Anya and I had both shuffled off this mortal coil then the children would go to the Whartons. They have a governess of their own, and so poor Maggie would be out of a job."

"Are the servants mentioned in your will at all?"

"Oh, good grief! No, they are not exactly aged and faithful retainers. The only one who has been with us a couple of years is Fisher, the butler, and he gets a token legacy only."

"And Miss Earnshaw? Another token legacy?"

Masterton shook his head. "She only came to us a few months ago, so I haven't had time to alter my will in her favour, even had I wanted to. Which I didn't." He smiled thinly. "Nothing to be made of that, Mr Holmes. And besides, though Maggie performs her duties as well as one would wish, I don't think she plans to remain a governess all her life. Rather than poison her employers, she'd be more likely to look for some personable young chap and ... oh." He broke off, and looked away.

"And poison the equally personable young wife, I think you were about to say?"

"Oh, forget that, Mr Holmes. It was a stupid, thoughtless thing to say. And besides, if Maggie ..." he stopped. "I'll consider my words very carefully, if you don't mind. If Maggie were to kill a wife in order to marry a widower, she would surely choose someone who would inherit his wife's money? Charles Gerard gains nothing by Emily's death."

"And did Miss Earnshaw know that?"

"Oh, yes. Maggie is more than a servant. Anya confides in her a good deal, and certainly Maggie knew about Emily's will." He hesitated. "Look here, Mr Holmes, I don't know if I'm speaking out of turn here, and I don't know how much you know about Maggie ..."

"We are aware that she and Mr Gerard had been ... ah, friends, back in London," said Holmes.

Masterton looked relieved. "So you know? Good. Well, then, if Charles and Maggie couldn't marry in England because neither of them has a bean, they could hardly hope to marry in the same beanless state here, could they?"

"It is a powerful pointer to Miss Earnshaw's total innocence, I agree," said Holmes. "One more question only, if it is not too much trouble. Was Miss Earnshaw in the house here when Charles Gerard called on the day his wife died?"

Masterton gave vent to a snort of sheer exasperation. Holmes held up a hand. "It is important," he said in his most soothing tone.

"Oh, very well, then. No, Maggie had gone out with the children, and with their nurse. I can call the nurse now, if you like, to verify that?"

"There is no need," said Holmes.

"No? And then they didn't get back until after I returned myself, and by that time Charles Gerard was long gone."

"Thank you, that is quite clear." Holmes made as if to stand up.

"One moment, Mr Holmes," said Masterton.

"Yes? You have thought of something?"

"Not as such. Masterton hesitated. "Look here, I hate to suggest such a thing, but ... well, the logical suspect when the wife is murdered must be the husband, or am I wrong?"

Holmes shook his head. "You are not wrong, alas."

"Well, then ... you seem to think that Charles cannot have done it, and I myself find it hard to accept such a notion. But I had no reason to kill my sister-in-law, and Anya had no reason to kill her sister, and Maggie Earnshaw certainly had no reason to kill anybody. Could it not have been Charles Gerard after all? Any discrepancies might be a clever, scheming man's way of confusing the investigation, pointing the finger at someone else. Anyone else."

"It is a thought," said Holmes, "and the motive for killing his wife? He did not stand to gain financially, as has been pointed out more than once."

"As to that, I cannot say," replied Masterton. "Perhaps there was another woman ... a woman as rich as, or richer than, Emily? Or perhaps the quarrel had something to do with it? The last straw, so to speak? Who can say just what may go on between a man and his wife?"

Ingham stirred. "He refuses to explain the quarrel, that's certain," he grunted.

Masterton nodded. "Significant, perhaps?"

"Perhaps," said Holmes. This time he did stand up. "I think that is all I have to ask for the moment, Mr Masterton. Oh, I forgot ... have you ever heard of a man named Cedric Masters?"

"What?" Masterton had pretty obviously not expected this. He started, and his face grew ashen. A palpable hit, thought I, if ever I saw one.

"Cedric Masters? You are not by any chance one Cedric Masters, are you?" asked Holmes.

Masterton recovered himself. "I told you earlier that I had a Bible somewhere in the place," said he. "I am perfectly willing to swear to you, here and now, that I am not Cedric Masters. Do you wish me to do that? No? In that event, you will, I am sure, excuse me. I shall ring for Fisher to show you out." And he suited the action to the words.

Chapter Eleven

What the Butler Saw

Fisher, the butler, sedate and unruffled as ever, escorted us to the front door. As he stepped across the threshold, Holmes held out a hand, and I saw the gleam of gold.

"Thank you, sir," said Fisher, so urbanely that it was almost a benediction.

Thank you," replied Holmes. He half turned to go, then looked back at the butler. "I wonder ... would it be inappropriate to have a quiet word with you? It is nothing that would smack of disloyalty to your employer, I assure you," he added, as Fisher frowned.

"Oh, in that event, sir." Fisher glanced behind him, saw that there was nobody about, and lowered his voice. "In that event, Mr Holmes, I shall perhaps have a few moments free around eleven-thirty. There's a little bar on the corner, nothing grand, where I sometimes pop in for a ... a breather, you know." And as there came a footfall in the passage, he said in a louder tone, "Thank you, sir. Good day to you," and shut the door in Holmes' face.

"An interesting character study," said Holmes, as we made our way to the carriage.

"The master, or the man?" asked Ingham quickly.

Holmes laughed. "Both," he replied. "Though I was thinking of Mrs Masterton."

"Oh." Ingham shrugged, and called out to his driver, who sat patiently on the carriage seat, "We'll make our own way back, thanks." As the carriage clattered away, he nodded down the road. "I know the bar that butler fellow meant. Not a very salubrious place, but I suppose it's handy for his purposes."

"Indeed," said Holmes. "He has, of course, a weakness for gin ... you spotted that? No? It has not developed to be detrimental to his duties as yet, but he needs to keep it in check."

"And do you think he will be able to tell us anything?" I asked. "You don't really suspect the butler, do you, Holmes?"

He laughed. "At the moment, he is probably as likely as anyone, for I cannot see for the life of me why the very obvious suspect would have committed the crime. No," he went on, before I could ask who this *very obvious suspect* might be, "no, it is less a matter of accusation than of information. Fisher, we are told, has been in the Masterton house longer than any of the other servants, so if anyone knows what is going on, he should."

"And you think there is something *going on*, as you put it?" asked Ingham quickly. "Do you suspect the Mastertons, or one of them, at any rate?"

"There are surely only three possibilities," said Holmes, as he reached the door of the little bar, and stood aside to let Ingham enter.

The place was certainly not the Raffles Hotel, I thought, as I glanced around. Tiny, dark and cramped, the only merit that I could see in it ... from Fisher's point of view ... was that it was handy for the Masterton house; and come to think of it, it was probably quite discreet, for it was not the sort of place

144

that a man owns up to patronizing. Quite suitable for a butler who was in the habit of popping out for a quick one, in fact. It was cool, though, or at any rate a touch cooler than the air outside.

We bought our drinks at the little bar ... no credit or waiters here ... and found a table in a far corner, although, as I say, the place was all but empty. And I have to add that it was soon emptier still, for some of the patrons took a look at Ingham and remembered urgent appointments elsewhere.

"Well, Holmes?" I said, with a touch of impatience.

"Well, then?"

"The three possibilities," I cried.

"Oh, those ... one, some peripatetic lunatic poisoned Mrs Gerard, quite at random."

"Nonsense!"

"I agree. Two, Charles Gerard poisoned his wife." He tilted his head to one side, and regarded Ingham and me, as if inviting comment.

"Motive?" asked Ingham doubtfully.

"Ah, that is the weak point. That, and Charles Gerard's curious behaviour with regard to the bottle of arsenic and the box of sugarplums."

"H'mm. I suppose the curious behaviour with the box was that he did nothing with it?" I said. "Yes, that is odd. Anyway, the third possibility is that it was one of the Mastertons, motive unknown yet again. And that's why we are sitting in this rather grimy den waiting for a butler who may, or may not, have something to tell us?"

"You sum it up tolerably well," said Holmes.

"There is a fourth possibility," said Ingham. "Though it may not be very sensible or likely. Mrs Gerard really could have committed suicide, and chosen a very confusing way of doing it."

"Very confusing indeed," said Holmes, and seemed about to add more, but was prevented from doing so by the appearance at the door of Fisher. Holmes stood up and shook the butler's hand. "Gin, was it not? And tonic?"

"Ah ... just a touch of bitters, sir, if it's all the same to you," replied Fisher. "They know how I take it," he added, as Holmes went to the bar.

"There you are," said Holmes, returning. "Please sit down, Mr Fisher." As the butler murmured his thanks and took a sip of his gin, Holmes went on, "Now, I told you that my questions would not involve any sort of disloyalty to your employers, and that is true enough. But, as a man who has been in the Masterton house several years, and as a shrewd and an observant man to boot, you might be very helpful to our investigations."

Fisher nodded. "I'm your man, sir. Ask away."

"Did the Mastertons ever quarrel?"

Fisher permitted himself a smile. "You're a bachelor, I take it, Mr Holmes? Yes, sir, there was an occasional little difference of opinion. Very little, and very occasional, for the master is an easy-going gentleman, and not too particular about details like the colour of curtains, or the exact number and position of chairs in a room, and that sort of thing which is the cause of many minor disputes 'twixt husband and wife. But when there is a trifling debate that has to be resolved, then Mr Masterton states his own opinion very forcefully, and then goes out and does just what Mrs Masterton says." And he took another sip of his gin, and allowed himself another smile at his brilliant originality.

"H'mm." Holmes forced a thin smile. "You have been with the family for some time; what is Mr Masterton's background?"

Fisher looked down at his glass.

"I ask out of mere curiosity," said Holmes casually.

"Oh, it is not that I am particularly reluctant to answer," said Fisher, "but rather that Mr Masterton is what you might call a 'man of mystery'. Not in any dark and sinister sense, or at any rate I don't think so, but just that nobody seems to know very much about him, where he comes from, what he did before he came to Singapore, that sort of thing. He has a trace of an Australian accent, at times. Or perhaps New Zealand or South Africa?"

"I see. Tell me, were you in the house when Mr Gerard called, the day Mrs Gerard died?"

Fisher's brow clouded. "I was, sir."

"Was Miss Earnshaw in the house?"

"No, sir, she and the nursemaid had taken the children out for some fresh air."

"Did you remain in the room whilst Mr Gerard was talking to the Mastertons?"

"Certainly not."

"Who else was in the house?"

Fisher thought. "The maids, of course. The cook and the kitchen boy."

"But none of them would have advised Mrs Masterton on her choice of a gift for Mrs Gerard? No, of course not," Holmes added quickly as Fisher frowned again, puzzled by the question.

Fisher coughed delicately, and consulted his watch. "Was there anything more you wished to know, sir? If not, I should be returning to my duties."

"Yes, of course. You have been most helpful," said Holmes – though his voice did not perhaps have the conviction to match the words.

Fisher shook hands all round, and nodded farewell.

As the door closed behind the butler, Holmes laughed. "Perhaps not quite as helpful as one might have wished," he told us. He raised an eyebrow. "Well, gentlemen? Any thoughts on the progress of the case thus far?"

"If we're to have a lengthy discussion, I need another drink," I told him. "What about you two?" I noted their requirements, and marched off to the bar. "Now," I said, when I had returned to my seat, "let us examine the sequence of events. Charles Gerard talks to Mrs Masterton, who gives him a box of sugarplums containing arsenic ..."

"Ahah!"

"Holmes? I trust you're not going to interrupt me at the end of every sentence?"

"Do we know that the arsenic was in the sweets at that stage?"

"No, I suppose not," I said gloomily. "Very well, then, Charles Gerard talks to Mrs Masterton, who gives him a box of sugarplums which may ... or may not ... contain arsenic." Holmes nodded his head at this. I went on, "Charles Gerard gives the box to his wife, and then leaves her alone again. He returns, to find his wife dead, a bottle of arsenic, a suicide note, and a glass on the table ... all of which he attempts to conceal ... oh!" I hesitated. "We have only his word that there was a note, but we do know that we found a bottle of arsenic where he said he put it."

Holmes nodded in satisfaction. "Admirably summed up, Watson. I would add only that the arsenic that was found in the sugarplums was confined to those with a centre ... that Mrs Gerard would avoid. So, any offers as to theories, then?"

"Well," I said, "I know that you have a weakness for the involved explanation, Holmes, so how's this? The sugarplums which Mrs Masterton gave to Gerard to give to Mrs Gerard ... sorry, that's confused, but you know what I mean ... the sugarplums were untouched, in every sense. Mrs Gerard herself set out to poison them, or some of them, in order to kill ... ah ..."

148

"Her sister, perhaps? Her husband?"

"I can't explain every last detail, of course," I said patiently. "But, in the course of poisoning the 'Violet Cremes' ... and that rather suggests that the intention was to kill Mrs Masterton, who had a weakness for that particular centre ... Mrs Gerard is unable to resist her craving for 'Walnut Whirls'." I paused here, to check that I had this the right way round. "Yes, that's right. She eats *those*, the 'Walnut Whirls', but in doing so accidentally transfers some of the arsenic to her mouth, and kills herself accidentally. The remains of the walnut sweets, and the arsenic, are thus both found in her body, so we all think they got there together, though in fact they got there more or less separately. How's that?" And I leaned back in triumph and sipped my drink.

"She would have to transfer a large amount ... accidentally," said Ingham.

"H'mm." I thought. "Possible, though?"

"And the note?" asked Holmes.

"Oh! The note, yes." I thought a moment. "Ah, but we only have Gerard's word that there ever was a note. He finds the body, the bottle ... no note ... thinks his wife has killed herself deliberately. Wanting to keep his wife's name unsullied, free of the taint of suicide, he hides the bottle, but not the box ... because, of course, he doesn't know that she's put poison in it ... and raises the alarm. But then later, when he himself is suspected of murder, he realizes that a bit of a slur on the family name is preferable to the gallows, so he seizes eagerly on your suggestion that there was a note, Holmes, and stresses the suicide aspect. Well?"

"Tolerably well, indeed," said Holmes, in a tone that was almost admiring. "In fact, you have pointed out something which had entirely escaped me."

"Oh!"

"Indeed." Holmes smiled at me. "And Mrs Gerard's motive for wanting her sister dead?"

"Ah, that is a puzzle. But then the motive is obscure with any theory," I pointed out. "If we knew the motive, we would know the killer."

"True enough," nodded Holmes. "Superintendent?"

"Charles Gerard," said Ingham shortly. "Poisons his wife ... whether using the box of sweetmeats or not, I couldn't say ... and arranges all the rest, the poison in the 'Violet Cremes' and the like, to obscure the facts. He knows he'll be the first one to be suspected, and he muddies the waters accordingly, by poisoning sweets he knows his wife won't eat, to make it look as if a stranger did it."

"Motive?"

"To be rid of his wife, probably got another woman tucked way."

Holmes smiled. "Now, I could agree, if Charles Gerard stood to inherit his wife's money. But he did not. If he wanted to marry this *other woman*, then why on earth did he not do so a year or more ago? He had as much money, or as little money, rather, as a bachelor as he does now as a widower. And remember, it was he who prompted his wife to dispose of her money in that odd ... relatively odd ... way that she did."

"Insurance!" I cried.

Holmes and Ingham stared at me.

"He might not inherit his wife's money, but what if he had insured her life for a large amount?" I went on. "That way, he collects a hefty chunk of cash, but no suspicion falls upon him."

"Excellent!" cried Holmes, rubbing his hands together.

"Is that the answer, then?" I asked.

"I do not think so."

"Oh."

"The problem is that being convicted of murder would rule out Gerard as a beneficiary, and he is, you will recall, at present under arrest on just that suspicion. The difficulty is that bottle, that dratted bottle which he hid in the dustbin," said Holmes. "If he wanted to throw suspicion upon Mrs Masterton, or anyone else, then surely he would conceal the bottle more carefully earlier on, and not wait until the very last minute and then use so clumsy a method? And why would he poison the 'Violet Cremes', thereby deflecting suspicion from Mrs Masterton, who knew that her sister disliked them? Any other flavour would have done, but not that. It makes very little sense. But I do not criticize you, Watson ... it is a possibility which genuinely had not occurred to me."

"It's kind of you to say so," I replied, a touch put out. "Well, Holmes, you have poured cold water on the theories advanced by Superintendent Ingham and myself, but what's your hypothesis?"

Holmes laughed, and shrugged his shoulders. "I confess that although I can see objections to your suggestions, I cannot think of any explanation that is free from very similar objections." He frowned. "It might be worth thinking about who would benefit, or stand to benefit, though. We know that Mrs Gerard was poisoned ... even if we do not know the precise means whereby the poison was administered. And we know that there was poison in the centres favoured by Mrs Masterton, and that Mrs Masterton ... unprompted by any third party ... gave the box of sugarplums to Charles Gerard. Suppose she had not done so? And she might easily not have done so ... indeed, the probability must be that she would not give the box away, that she herself would have opened the box and eaten the poisoned sweets. Now, if both Mrs Gerard and Mrs Masterton had died, who would gain?"

"Derek Masterton!" cried Ingham and I with one voice.

151

Holmes nodded. "He had the opportunity ... we are told that he was out of the house, ostensibly on business. And Charles Gerard had left his wife alone in their rooms. Masterton could have gone round to the Gerards' lodgings, offered Mrs Gerard a drink ... perhaps a remedy for her headache? He poisons her, leaves the note ... a portion of a letter sent by Mrs Gerard to Mrs Masterton, let us say ... and goes about his lawful occasions."

"Wait just a moment, though," I said. "If Mrs Gerard had died first, her money would have gone to Mrs Masterton; and if Mrs Masterton had then died, Derek Masterton would inherit everything. But suppose that Mrs Masterton had eaten the sugarplums, the poisoned ones at any rate, before Mrs Gerard had been poisoned? Wouldn't Mrs Gerard's will then be invalid, and the money go to Charles Gerard?"

Holmes nodded. "It is an interesting legal point. But then Masterton would know that his wife was still alive when he left the house, so he would think that he had time to poison Mrs Gerard before Mrs Masterton ate the sugarplums. He could not guess that she would give them away."

"He'd see them in Mrs Gerard's room," I objected.

Holmes shook his head. "How could he possibly know it was the same box? He was not in the house when his wife gave the box to Gerard, remember. And more to the point, it may not all have been about money. Suppose, let us say, that Derek Masterton had somehow got wind of the fact that Mrs Gerard had hired Mr Ellis to look into his ... Masterton's ... past?"

"Oh, you mean that Masterton might have been concerned that Mrs Gerard would learn that he was actually Cedric Masters, and a thief?" I said.

Holmes shook his head. "I mean that Derek Masterton might have been concerned lest Mrs Gerard should learn that he meant to kill his own wife," he replied.

"Good Lord!"

Superintendent Ingham stood up. "You make out a convincing case against Derek Masterton," he said.

"And yet there are objections," said Holmes. "Many objections."

"For all the objections, I think that another word with Mr Derek Masterton would not come amiss," said Ingham, and led the way to the door.

We had gone perhaps halfway back towards the Masterton house, when something of a commotion attracted our attention. A door banged, there was an indistinct shout, followed by another bang of a door ... and all this was pretty clearly emanating from the very house we were making for, the Masterton house. We each increased our pace.

Fisher, no longer quite as sedate as of old, emerged from the drive at a run, followed by a pretty young Chinese maidservant. Fisher stopped at the edge of the road, looked round wildly at the crowd, spotted us, waved, shouted, and then – despite the heat, which was now noticeable – set off running towards us. We naturally ran to meet him, to see what might be wrong.

"Doctor!" he cried, as soon as he was close enough to be properly heard. "Doctor Watson, come quickly, sir, if you please."

"What, then?"

"Mr Masterton, sir. He's been poisoned."

Chapter Twelve

Sherlock Holmes Explains

"Feeling better now?" I asked Derek Masterton.

He nodded. "Yes, thanks to you, Doctor."

We had, as you will have gathered, got there just in time. The poison was not corrosive, and I had managed to induce him to get rid of most of it. Now, very wan and shaken, he was propped up in bed in one of the guest rooms. Mrs Masterton, roused from her own fitful slumbers in the master bedroom by the commotion, stood in the doorway, wrapped in a dressing gown, and regarded the proceedings in a stunned silence.

Holmes tapped me on the shoulder. "Arsenic?" he asked.

"We should get Doctor Oong's opinion, of course," I answered, "but it certainly looks that way to me."

"Just so. Mr Masterton," Holmes said to my patient, "are you strong enough to tell us what happened?"

"Oh, I'm strong enough for anything," replied Masterton with a valiant attempt at a smile. "But as for telling you what happened, I'm blessed if I know myself."

"Well, tell us what happened after you threw ... that is, after we left the house."

Masterton nodded. "I stamped about the place for a while, generally cursing you, and this whole damnable affair. I looked in on Anya, and she seemed to be resting. Then I thought I'd buckle down to some work, so I got out some papers that I needed to examine. Only I couldn't concentrate, this dreadful business has unsettled me, and shaken me more badly than I like to admit. I thought a drink might possibly help ... I don't usually, not at this time of day, but I thought it was justified under the circumstances. I poured myself a drink, then ..."

"Of what?" asked Holmes.

"Oh, whisky. I ..."

"Does anyone else in the house drink whisky?"

Masterton frowned. "I don't see why that matters, but, no. Anya never touches spirits, and Fisher prefers a drop of gin, though he thinks I don't know."

Fisher, standing discreetly to one side, started slightly at this revelation, and strove, not altogether successfully, to hide a smile.

"I see. Please go on," said Holmes.

"Nothing much more to tell, I'm afraid," said Masterton. "I took a hefty pull at my drink, and I remember thinking that it tasted a little odd. Then I felt sick and dizzy, and only just managed to ring the bell for Fisher here before I collapsed."

Holmes looked at Fisher, who nodded. "I came when the master rang, sir, and found him slumped all of a heap on the floor," said Fisher. "I tried to move him, realized that he needed a medical man, and ran out into the road. Then ... heaven be praised ... I saw you gentlemen strolling in this direction. The rest you know," he added.

Ingham said, "Where do we go from here, Mr Holmes?"

Holmes glanced at Fisher, who correctly interpreted the look and said to Masterton, "If there's nothing more, sir?"

"No, thank you, Fisher." Masterton hesitated, and then told Mrs Masterton, "And if you would please excuse us, Anya? I'd like a word with these gentlemen in private. Nothing to worry about, my dear," he added, as she looked understandably anxious. "Anyway, shouldn't you be resting? Yes, I know it's a nuisance, but Doctor Watson is here to look after me now, so you just get your maid to help you back to bed."

I escorted Mrs Masterton back to her own room, and handed her over to her maid. Then I hurried back to see what Derek Masterton might have to say for himself.

He sat up in bed as I entered the room. "Just close the door there, would you, Doctor? Not that I suspect anyone ..." And when I had complied with his request, he told us to sit where we could. Holmes and Ingham found chairs and drew them close, while I perched on the foot of the bed.

"Now, Mr Masterton?" said Ingham.

Masterton managed a weak grin. "Just a couple of points I'd like to get straight, Superintendent. Both a touch awkward, I'm afraid."

"Oh?"

"Yes. First off, you asked me if I was Cedric Masters?"

"And are you?"

Masterton shook his head. "I said I wasn't, and I'm not. But I am his brother, Derek Masters."

"Ah!" Ingham sat up at this.

Masterton went on, "You'll know the story about Cedric? Our old father was cheated by a plausible crook, and Cedric decided ... rightly or wrongly ... that since the law couldn't, or wouldn't, act, he would. He set out to take back what he thought was his. Oh, I know," he went on as Ingham seemed about to speak, "you'll say that you cannot condone what he did, and so on and so forth. Well, I perhaps see things differently. I have my own ideas as to the rights and wrongs of it, and you have yours. That's neither here nor there. The important thing is that Cedric came to see me, right after the robbery. I had a farm of sorts, a cattle ranch out in the back country, though nobody ever knew I was Cedric's brother, I think. Well, he turned up there, one fine evening, and I took him in. What else could I do?

"He was wounded, pretty badly, by a police bullet. I wanted to call a doctor, but Cedric said no, he hadn't long to live anyway, and even if he could be saved he didn't want to die in prison, or on the gallows, especially not for killing a crook who so richly deserved to die. If he had to go, he'd sooner go under my roof. And go he did, but not before he'd made me promise to return as much of the money to its rightful owners as was humanly possible, and keep only what was rightly due to us ... to him, and then to me as his heir, though there was no written will or any nonsense of that sort."

"And you did so?" asked Holmes.

Masterton nodded. "The Australian police will tell you that the money ... some of it, at any rate ... was returned anonymously to those who'd been cheated of it. That was my work. I couldn't hope to contact all of them, because some had died, some had moved house, and some I simply didn't know about. But I did what I could. I'd sold the farm by then, and moved away, and eventually landed up here."

"And your brother?" I asked.

Masterton's face clouded. "He didn't make it," he said. "I buried him out in the bush, where nobody would ever find him. Read from the Bible and everything ... that's all he'd have wanted or needed, and the same goes for me."

"Well," said Holmes, "it is not for me to judge your brother ... or you. Not for the old crime, anyway. Superintendent?"

Ingham shook his head. "Cedric Masters may have been wanted in Australia, but we never had anything against him here in Singapore. As for you, Mr Masterton ..." and he emphasized the name slightly ..."the Australian police might perhaps make a case for failing to report your brother's death, or, more serious, for receiving stolen money. But that would only be if they found you, and I, for one, don't plan to tell them."

"Thank you, sir," said Masterton.

"But," added Ingham, "there remains the little matter of Mrs Gerard's death. Now, this latest bit of business," and he gestured at Masterton, lying there in bed, "does rather tend to show that you had nothing to do with Mrs Gerard's death, but for all that, I'd like to make sure."

"But I was poisoned as well," cried Masterton.

Ingham shook his head. "You knew Fisher was in the house, and were not so badly affected that you could not ring the bell to summon help. A clever man, knowing that he was suspected of using poison, might take a small dose himself, if he knew there was no real danger, in order to make it look as if he were a victim rather than the murderer."

Masterton shook his head in despair.

I said, "Look here, Superintendent, had I ... we ... not got here when we did, Mr Masterton wouldn't be alive to answer any questions. I'll swear to that."

"H'mm." Ingham looked baffled. Then, "Mr Masterton, it seems that I owe you an apology, sir."

"Accepted."

"But tell me," Ingham went on, "what was the second thing you were going to tell us?"

"Ah, yes." Masterton levered himself upright, and gazed earnestly at the Superintendent. "We have a cat, you see."

"Ah. That is nice."

Masterton laughed. "No, I'm not rambling. It's a very old cat, and sometimes gets a bit lethargic on a morning, won't get out of her basket. In that case, I give her a spoonful of my whisky ... an extravagance, I know, but she's part of the family, you see ... in a saucer of milk. I did that this morning, and she's capering about like a kitten."

"H'mm. Meaning that the whisky was poisoned in the last few hours, then?"

Masterton nodded. "And nobody ... except, that is, Fisher ... has left the house. That means that the poison must still be here. At any rate the bottle or container. Unless, of course, Fisher did it, and disposed of the bottle when he went out just now."

Ingham shook his head. "Could have been wrapped in a twist of paper, and a match put to it," he grumbled. He stood up. "Still, it would be neglecting our duty not to look. Mr Holmes, Doctor, can I rely upon your assistance?"

We made our way out on to the landing, and Ingham closed the bedroom door behind him. He glanced round, and lowered his voice. "Well, Mr Holmes? A bit too prompt in suggesting that we search for the poison, d'you think?"

"H'mm. Perhaps. But, as you said yourself, it would be silly not to look." Holmes smiled grimly. "And I would wager that I know where to look first."

"Oh? And where might that be, then?"

"In Mrs Masterton's room," said Holmes.

"Mrs ..." I began, but Holmes silenced me with a look.

"No need to let all Singapore know, Watson," he said with some irritation.

"Sorry, Holmes. But, really, do you think that Mrs ..."

"I think it would be as well to look there first," he repeated calmly. "And perhaps politic to collect Mrs Masterton's maid before we rush in there."

We found the maid, who looked first frightened, then puzzled and then angry. We asked her to take us to Mrs Masterton's room. The maid tapped on the door, and looked in. "Beg pardon, ma'am, but the policemen would like to see you."

"Oh?" came Mrs Masterton's voice from inside the room. "Show them in, please."

The maid stood aside, and Ingham led us into the room. "Sorry to disturb you again, Mrs Masterton," he began, "but the fact is ... well ..."

Holmes glanced round the room, gave a little nod, and darted over to the dressing table, where a large box stood. "Your jewel box, I think, Mrs Masterton?"

"Why, yes. I like to have them where I can see them ... a foolish fancy, but a common one." Mrs Masterton looked frankly bewildered.

Holmes nodded. "A very obvious hiding place, you will agree?" he told Ingham and me. And before we could reply, he had opened the lid of the box and pulled out a little blue glass poison bottle, the duplicate of the one he had found in the dustbin earlier.

"But ... but I didn't put that there!" cried Mrs Masterton.

Holmes bowed to her. "You need not concern yourself, madam," he told her. "I shall attend to everything, now that we have this last piece of the puzzle." And he ushered Ingham and me out on to the landing again.

"Admit it, now, Holmes," I said, "you knew that bottle was in there."

"No, Watson," said he, very serious, "I assure you that I did not know, or not for certain. But as I say, it is a very obvious hiding place; just the sort of place someone might put the bottle knowing it would be found by a very cursory search, and wanting it to be found."

"You mean someone put that there to incriminate Mrs Masterton?"

"I do. Why, it is ludicrous to suppose that she would poison her husband and conceal the bottle of poison in her own room."

Ingham frowned. "A clever bluff? Knowing that we'd think it ludicrous?"

Holmes shook his head. He turned to the maid, who was standing there open-mouthed. "Tell me, had Mrs Masterton left her room since you saw her to it that first time?"

"No, sir. I've been across the way, right up until all the fuss with the poor master, and the mistress never stirred from her room."

Holmes nodded. "Thank you. Moreover," he went on to Ingham and me, "I know for a fact that the bottle was not there earlier, for when we helped Mrs Masterton to her room the first time, I took advantage of the fuss that you were making of her to look into that box, and it contained nothing that it should not contain."

"Why on earth did you do that?" asked Ingham.

Holmes shrugged. "Force of habit. As I say, so very obvious." He looked at me. "Watson, do you assure me that Derek Masterton was in danger of his life from poison? He could not merely have given himself a small dose to appear ill?"

I shook my head. "It was genuine, or I'm no doctor, Holmes."

"In that event, we must arrest the real culprit." Holmes turned to the little maid, who was regarding us with complete astonishment. "Which is Miss Earnshaw's room?"

"Miss Earnshaw, sir? Why, it's this way," and she led us down the corridor, up a short flight of steps, and indicated door.

Holmes tapped on the door, and there was a curious muffled sound from within. "Miss Earnshaw?" called

Holmes. "I must ask you to open the door, madam." And, when there came no answer, he opened the door himself.

"How dare you burst in like this?" Miss Earnshaw, flushed of face, stared at us from the other side of her bed. She had evidently been packing, for a suitcase lay open on the bed, and there were clothes and effects scattered about.

"Not going anywhere, are you, miss?" asked Ingham.

Before Miss Earnshaw could reply, Holmes had called out, "Careful, Watson," as Miss Earnshaw grabbed a pair of scissors and lunged towards me.

Without thinking, I picked up a candlestick that stood on the dressing table, and brought it down with an audible crack on her wrist. Unsporting and ungentlemanly, I know, but it isn't every day a man is attacked with scissors, and I had no experience of how best to react.

I attended to Miss Earnshaw's wrist, before Superintendent Ingham found some handcuffs for it, and its companion. As she was marched off, I asked her, "But why?"

She gave me a look full of hatred. "You fool," she hissed at me. "You damned fool!"

* * *

"Am I a fool, Holmes?" I asked a little later, as we sat with Superintendent Ingham in the Long Bar of the Raffles Hotel.

"If you are," said Ingham, "so am I, for I haven't a clue as to why she did it."

"Has she said nothing?" asked Holmes.

Ingham shook his head. "Not a word. So, Mr Holmes, it's rather up to you to clear things up."

"Oh, that is soon done," said Holmes, in his usual offhand manner. "She meant to kill both Mrs Gerard and Mrs Masterton. Mrs Masterton with the poisoned sweets ... that Miss Earnshaw did not, of course, know would be given away

... and Mrs Gerard with a dose of arsenic administered in a glass of something. I suspect Miss Earnshaw had called upon Mrs Gerard, asked about her headache, sympathized, offered a *special remedy*, mixed it, and ..."

I shook my head. "But Miss Earnshaw was with the nursemaid and the Masterton children."

Holmes looked at Ingham. The Superintendent said, "Ah, yes. It seems the nursemaid has a young man. Miss Earnshaw was very obliging, said she would see to the children while the nursemaid had a little walk and talk with this chap. And then when the nursemaid returned, Miss Earnshaw asked her to return the favour, said she had some business to attend. Of course, the nursemaid never suspected anything out of the way, and equally of course she never mentioned this little *arrangement* to the police."

"Well, that explains that," I said. "But then, arsenic is not a fast acting sort of thing. There are symptoms, unpleasant symptoms. Why did Mrs Gerard not call for help?"

"Ah," said Holmes, embarrassed. "I can only think that she did not call for help simply because Miss Earnshaw was there, offering her cologne, promising to call a doctor, that sort of thing."

"You mean that Miss Earnshaw sat there and watched her die?" I cried, aghast.

"I do," said Holmes grimly.

"But," asked Ingham, "what about the poisoned sweets, then? Was there poison in the walnut centres?"

Holmes shook his head. "I think not. Miss Earnshaw poisoned the violet centres, to kill Mrs Masterton. She did not, I believe, also poison the walnut centres, for she could not know that the box would be passed on as it was. She left it in Mrs Gerard's room because she did not realize that it was the same box. No, I think she poisoned Mrs Gerard with a drink, a glass of something for her headache."

164

"Dreadful," I said with a shudder.

Holmes nodded. "I do not think she is a very nice person," he added.

"To say the least. And Doctor Oong naturally assumed that the poison was administered in the walnut sweets."

"And we did not think to question it," said Holmes ruefully. "An object lesson in not taking things at their face value, Watson."

"Indeed. But, Holmes, what was the point of it all? To marry Charles Gerard, I suppose? But what about the money? As we keep saying, if they could not afford to marry in London, then how could they hope to do so in Singapore?"

"Ah, you ask an interesting question," said Holmes with a smile. "Two points come to mind. First, if the scheme had worked, there was a logical suspect in Derek Masterton. Now, it may have been that the police might not have arrested anyone, that the Superintendent here would have thought the case insufficient against him. In that event, I suspect that Miss Earnshaw would have offered comfort to the grieving widower, and would in a relatively short while have become the second Mrs Masterton."

"But you just said that she wanted to marry Charles Gerard," I said, puzzled.

Holmes smiled. "How long do you think Derek Masterton would have lived?" he asked me.

"Good Lord! But suppose the police had arrested him for the double murder? What then?"

"Ah, then Miss Earnshaw would, I think, have suggested to the obliging Mr Wharton that Mr Masterton's will was made before Emily Cardell got married. What more natural than for the deceased wife's deceased sister's widower ... Charles Gerard, that is ... to take custody of the children? And the money, of course."

"But the capital would go to the children," I pointed out.

"If they survived."

"Good Heavens!"

Holmes nodded. But you have not heard my second point, Watson," he added with smile.

"And what is that?"

"That it may not have been about the money at all. We have heard that Charles Gerard is an independent sort of fellow; is it too difficult to suppose that he had married Emily Cardell because he loved her, rather than for her money? He asked her not to leave him the cash, remember. He may ... unpalatable though the notion may have been to Miss Earnshaw ... he may have omitted to propose marriage to Miss Earnshaw not because they were both poor, but because he simply did not love her."

"Oh. I never thought of that!" I nodded. "I see, now. Simple, of course."

"Of course," agreed Holmes.

Ingham asked, "So Miss Earnshaw faked Mrs Gerard's suicide, with the bottle ... the first bottle ... and the note, which was a page, or part of a page, from a letter from Mrs Gerard to Miss Earnshaw, asking forgiveness for pinching ... as she saw it ... her friend's gentleman friend? Yes, like Doctor Watson, I see it now Mr Holmes has explained it. But why leave the poisoned sugarplums there? To confuse us?"

Holmes shrugged. "She did not know it was the same box, of course, or she would have taken it away, so as *not* to confuse us. And then finally, when things went wrong because Charles Gerard tried to conceal the suicide, as he believed it to be, Miss Earnshaw, feeling the hand of the law upon her lace collar, or on that of her lover, tried to make us suspect Mrs Masterton, by poisoning Mr Masterton and placing the bottle in his wife's room, when Mrs Masterton left the room to see what the commotion was. Does that explain everything?"

I nodded. "I think so, Holmes. Oh … that quarrel the Gerards had?"

Holmes looked at Ingham. "Superintendent? Was that ever cleared up?"

Ingham laughed. "Yes, Charles Gerard explained, a little shame-faced. Apparently his wife wanted to move to her sister's, or to the 'Raffles'. He wanted to stay where they were for the time being."

"And that was all?" asked Holmes.

"You never married, then, sir?"

Holmes laughed. "Never, and if that's the sort of trivial thing that a man and wife argue over …"

I laughed with him. "You miss a lot of good things as well, though, Holmes. Anyway, everything's clear now. Another successful case."

"Indeed. And now, perhaps, we can do what you planned for us all along, Watson, and have a good long rest here at the 'Raffles'."

I gazed at him. "You saw through our scheme, then? Yes, of course." I stretched luxuriously. "Well, Holmes, you can rest all you want to, but I have a busy night ahead of me."

"Oh? Going to a party, then?"

"Not a bit of it. I shall be sitting up on the veranda with a rifle, and a glass of something or the other. Not sure just what, but it'll probably contain a high proportion of gin."

Sherlock Holmes will return
in a new adventure

**Sherlock Holmes
and the
Morphine Gambit**

by

Jason Cooke